Beauty isn't everything. Beneath Simone's long fake hair, phony smile, and saline booty is a web of trickery, lies, and murder. After being attacked by Jimmy, Simone's web of lies begins to violently unravel. One by one, her skeletons are falling out of the closet and revealing her true colors. While Simone fights to keep the man and life that she stole, Chance is fighting desperately to keep his life with Gia. Amidst the hot and steamy passion, which builds between Gia and Chance like a scorching inferno, is the fear of Chance being locked away for the rest of his life. After a visit from the new detective assigned to Aeysha's murder case, Eboni is intent on making Omari see the truth about Simone and her wicked ways.

In Secrets of a Side Bitch 3, everyone is forced to come clean and see their true involvement in Aeysha Walker's murder. And finally Simone is forced to make a decision – either face the aftermath of her destruction or run away from the man that she fought so hard to get.

FEMISTRY PRESS PUBLICATIONS
A self-publishing entity
info@femistrypress.net
wholesale@femistrypress.net
www.jessica-n-watkins.com

This is a work of fiction. Names, characters, places, and incidents are products of the author's imagination or are used fictitiously and are not to be assumed as real. Any resemblance to actual events, locales, organizations, or persons, living or dead, is entirely coincidental.

All rights reserved. No part of this book may be used or reproduced in any manner whatsoever without written permission, except in case of brief quotations embodied in critical articles and reviews. For additional information address Femistry Press.

Femistry Press Paperback Printing
Smart Black Rich Publications Digital Printing

Cover Art by TSPub Creative

Copyright @ 2013 by Jessica N. Watkins
Printed in the USA.

If you purchased this book without a cover, you should be aware that this book is stolen property. It was reported as "unsold and destroyed" to the publisher, and neither the author nor publisher has received any payment for this "stripped book".

Previously on…

SECRETS OF A SIDE BITCH

Omari

"What's up, Capone?"

"We got a problem, boss."

I wasn't in the mood to hear no shit like that. It was too early in the morning for dumb shit.

"What's the problem?"

"It's a thief in the crib."

"A thief? Which crib? What's missing?"

"Three bricks are missing from the spot in Riverdale."

My stomach did three somersaults so serious that I got a little sick. Three bricks were worth at least ninety-thousand dollars on the street.

"Somebody broke in?"

As Capone replied, "Hell nah," I went ahead and got out of bed. It was obvious that I was gone have to hit the block much earlier than usual. "When Chance told me that the count was off, first thing I assumed was Ching. But them niggas wouldn't come in here for just three bricks."

"Hell nah they wouldn't. You think Chance grabbed them?"

"Hell nah, man. He don't come off to me as that type of dude."

"Paula?"

"She swear to God it wasn't her."

I moaned and groaned in frustration. This shit wasn't cool. It put me in a fucked up position because whoever stole the shit had to get dealt with. The only nigga I was focused on dealing with at the moment was Ching, who was still somewhere hiding. He hadn't been to any of his spots. Black, Smoke, and Burt ran most of his errands. Ching had disappeared.

Ching wasn't a punk. He wasn't a runner. He wasn't the type of nigga to just let me get away with shooting at him and stealing from him. I knew at some point he would resurface. I had to find him before he found me.

"You at the spot?"

"Hell yea."

"Be there in a minute."

I hung up, threw the cell on the bed, and just paced with my head in my hands. I did not want to deal with this shit. Everybody that worked for me, I fucked with heavy. I trusted every block boy and every hype with my life. They were loyal.

But they knew me not to be some crazy trigger happy savage. So it was possible that one of them was taking my kindness for weakness.

"What's wrong, babe?"

Simone came into the room wearing a black long sleeve sweater maxi dress that fell to her ankles and over a pair of Christian Louboutin boots that cost me three thousand dollars. Her pudgy stomach stuck out of the cashmere.

She really wasn't on my good side either. She went to the doctor without me again, and it really pissed me the fuck off. She was treating me like I was some nigga too busy to be a part of my child's life, when she knew that I would go over and beyond to do any and everything for my children.

She watched me pace curiously.

"Somebody stole some work out the spot," I told her, answering her curiosity.

Her eyes bucked as she took her usual seat at the vanity. Her hair was already done. Now she was doing her makeup.

"Who do you think did it and when?"

"Ain't no tellin'. We only go in the stash when we gotta make more packs."

"Your people wouldn't steal from you."

"I didn't think so, but apparently somebody did."

"Maybe it was Tiana."

Though they had ruled out abuse and stopped investigating Tiana and her boyfriend, I still hadn't been fucking with her. I heard from her brother, Fred, that she felt some type of way about that. But he was so loyal to me that he was also mad at Tiana for having that dude in my crib anyway.

I pondered over the thought as Simone continued to convince me. "She still has a key."

"It would honestly make me feel better if she was the one that did it. At least it wouldn't be one of my people turning on me."

Chance

It was weird as hell looking at Lexington House. I hadn't seen it since I left for transitional housing last year. It's funny how sitting in that parking lot felt like being at home.

Back then, I hated being there. I hated my life. I was lost.

At that moment, I would have given anything to go back to that place in life. Now I was realizing that my past was a cakewalk compared to the shit that I was facing now.

Ever since leaving Lexington, I had hit roadblock after roadblock.

The biggest boldest dirtiest roadblock in my life came walking towards my car in a black sweater dress. I noticed that she was either pregnant or had gained some weight.

When she opened the door and sat in my car, the smell of Acqua Di Gioia overpowered the smell of weed that Capone left in there earlier that day.

"Here," was all that she said as she handed me a plastic bag. It was heavy. I looked in it curiously and immediately recognized the bricks.

"Tuh," I grunted. This chick was unbelievable. "So you the one stole them bricks."

"Yes, for you. That's worth almost a hundred thousand dollars. Now you can leave."

I wasn't excited. Had she bought these bricks with her own money, this would be great. If I took these three bricks and left town, I would never be able to come back to Chicago, due to the price on my head that Omari and Capone would put there because they would assume that my disappearance was due to me stealing from them. I couldn't just go to Minnesota either. I would have to go so far that word of my come up and whereabouts didn't make it back to the Chi.

"Was Omari at the spot when you left?"

I shook my head, barely paying attention to what she was saying because my thoughts were taking over.

"Where is he? Do you know?"

"Him and Capone moved all the product out of the spot in Riverdale. They takin' it out south."

I sighed heavily as the bricks lay on my lap.

Simone saw me contemplating. "Chance, this isn't money, but this is your opportunity to leave and start all over. You can work for yourself. You don't have to stand on some block all winter anymore."

I didn't want to leave. I liked my life. I had done some pretty terrible things, but I finally liked my life. I liked my homies. The thought of just walking away from Gia tugged at my heart, but knowing that I was also walking away from that pussy damn near brought a tear to my eye.

Noticing my reluctance, Simone began to beg me to leave. "Please, Chance."

She slipped her hand softly on my thigh. I immediately smacked her arm so hard that her hand flew off and she screeched out in pain.

"Nigga…"

She called herself getting hype, but my anger far surpassed hers. I was damn near in the passenger seat with her as my rage poured out of me like smoke as I pointed aggressively at her face.

"You lyin' ass, bitch! You can stop playing these fucking mind games! Don't fucking touch me!"

Simone just sat there, coolly and innocent, as always.

Finally, my anger subsided. Reluctantly, I put the

bricks in the backseat on the floor. The happiness in Simone couldn't be hidden, no matter how hard she tried to act nonchalantly at my conceding to yet another one of her devious moves.

"Get the fuck out of my car, Simone."

"Are you leaving?"

"GET THE FUCK OUT!"

The audacity of this bitch sent my anger off the meter. I reached over her, opened the door, and started pushing her so hard that she had to get out of the car before she fell out. It took everything in me not to beat the shit out of her like I wanted to. She had taken everything from me and still was. I was still a pawn in her game just to get another man.

I was mad at her for being a conniving bitch, but I was angrier with myself for being so weak.

I was putting the car in reverse before she was even able to slam the car door. Then I sped off and out of the parking lot. I never wanted to see that bitch again.

SIMONE

I let out a big sigh of relief as I watched Chance speed out of the parking lot. I didn't give a fuck how mad he got, he needed to leave town. Though he didn't tell me that he was leaving or when, I knew that he was. He was young, but he was far from stupid.

Now that Chance was out of the way, I had one more trick up my sleeve before I headed home. I noticed how much better I felt as I drove towards the suburbs. Getting Chance out of Chicago had been such a burden. However, the burden was lifting rapidly by the second.

When I pulled up in front of the house in Riverdale, I spotted Fred on post.

I rolled my window down and asked, "Is Paula in there?"

"Yea, Simone. She in there. What's up?"

"Tell her to come here."

Then I hurriedly rolled my window back up to block out the cold. It was almost April, but it was still barely in the high forties during the day. It always took Chicago a long time to convert from winter to spring.

About a minute passed before Paula came

bouncing out of the house. Her hair had grown longer, but it was unkempt. It was dirty blond hair that fell almost to her butt, but it was literally dirty and appeared to be greasy. She was an older hype. Paula had to be in her forties. Because of the drugs, she looked to be in her late fifties. Skin that was once clear and pink was now filthy with needle marks, bruises, and deterioration from the drugs. Her body was frail and looked weak and sickly.

When she got in my car, I could smell the funk all over her. She probably hadn't showered in days. I rolled down the window with my nose turned up.

"Hey, Simone."

She shivered from the cold. She didn't even have on a coat. She had on the same worn and dirty Abercrombie hoodie that she'd worn all winter.

"I have a job for you. You aren't going anywhere anytime soon, are you?"

I was the one that put Omari up on Paula. I often times saw her begging downtown around my condo. One time, I even saw her going through the trash. I knew that she was on drugs, so when Omari needed the trap out south cleaned, or any other odd job, I told him about Paula. Then she eventually started cooking and cutting heroin for him, amongst other things.

The pay was lucrative for her, but hypes did shit like disappear without notice. They fell off the map here and there, ran away, or got themselves clean out of nowhere.

"I don't plan on it," she said with a laugh. "What kind of job?"

"I need you to help me steal a baby."

Paula laughed initially, but when she saw that I hadn't cracked a smile, she took me seriously.

"What the fuck?"

"You heard me."

When Omari told me that his sister was having a c-section, that's when it dawned on me. I could take Erica's baby. They were siblings, so, hopefully, the baby would look similar to Omari; hopefully even having those genetically strong gray eyes.

I had it all planned out, so I shared with Paula the plan that I had been weaving together for weeks. Since Erica was scheduled to have her c-section in a few weeks when she was seven months, I would tell Omari that I was scheduled out of town for a speaking engagement with my job far away in Texas somewhere, too far for Omari to get to in time when I called him frantically saying that I was going into premature labor. Instead, I would be in Indianapolis, waiting on Erica to leave the hospital with her baby. Then Paula would car jack her, taking the baby with her.

Given the distance in Erica and Blood's relationship, I assumed that I could pull this off. I didn't even know if Erica knew that I was supposedly pregnant. The way that things were playing out, she and Omari would never see each other again, so I could get away with this if I played it ever so carefully.

I know I sounded insane and irrational. Even Paula looked at me like I was a lunatic. I kinda *had* gone insane. Trying to come up with a way to get myself out of this impractical ass pregnancy lie that I had spun was driving me absolutely crazy. But the more Omari lovingly touched my belly and called me the mother of his child, I could not bear to take another child from him by lying and saying that I lost this baby because I would not be able to realistically produce one.

"You are crazy as hell, Simone," Paula replied shaking her head and nervously looking out of the window.

I grabbed her arm and snatched her towards me, making her give me her full attention. My eyes looked beady, scary, and obsessed. I knew it, because Paula was cringing in fear.

I needed Paula's help because I definitely couldn't pull this off on my own. Erica would spot me for sure. But she would never know who Paula was. I wasn't scared of Paula telling. She loved that dope too much to risk losing her spot in Omari's kitchen.

Holding her arm in my hand and digging my acrylic nails into her weakening skin, I threatened her. "Crazy or not, you will help me, or I will tell Omari that I saw you stealing those three bricks."

Paula gasped. "No, I didn't!"

"As far as I know, you did."

I aggressively released her arm and she rubbed it in agony. "Okay. All right. I'll help you."

GIA

Chance and I were at the White Palace having breakfast. It was two in the morning. I had just left Sunset, along with Chance, who'd spent his evening kicking it there. Chance was at Sunset so much that the bouncers and bartenders knew him well, so being there was like hanging with friends at this point, not just going to see some ass and titties.

Things had gotten better between me and Chance since my outburst a few days ago when he couldn't keep an erection. I guess he peeped how he was acting and redirected his anger. He was back to his normal, attentive, and caring self.

Things were finally getting back to normal.

So I thought and so I was feeling, until Chance dropped a bomb on me.

Sitting across from me playing in his omelet, he told me, "I need to leave town for a minute."

"Excuse me?"

He hadn't said that he was taking a trip or making a run for Omari. This sounded permanent, so I instantly got an attitude.

"I said that I need to leave…"

"I heard you! Why?"

He ran his hand over his head and continued to play in his food without answering me.

"Chance."

I couldn't believe that he was acting like this. I figured that whatever it was that had been bothering him, whatever it was that was making him run, didn't have anything to do with me. We weren't in love, but I hoped that the time we spent together would at least deserve some sensitivity and respect.

"Chance, answer me."

"I can't." He finally looked me in my eyes. I noticed how weary and tired they were. He was back to being the sad and lonely boy that I met at the strip club a few months ago.

"You can't?" But I didn't care how weary or tired he was. I had given him what I hadn't been willing to give any man in years–*me*. He convinced me to let my wall down, to let him in, to trust him, and now he was too much of a pussy to handle whatever business he needed to, rather than walking away and just fucking leaving me here to wallow in grief.

"When are you leaving?"

"My flight leaves in a couple of hours."

My eyes fell out of my sockets. "A couple of hours?! How long have you known that you were leaving?"

"Not that long. I just got the ticket yesterday." He noticed my tears and sighed. "Are you crying?"

"Hell yes, I'm crying. You've been laying up in my crib and fucking me, but didn't even have the decency to tell me that you were leaving."

"We're not even in a relationship, Gia."

"And?!"

"I didn't mean it like that. I meant, I didn't think you would care this much. I didn't think it would hurt you."

I was livid. Literally, my heart was beating so fast with anger and shock that I was becoming short of breath. "You didn't think it would hurt me? Are you serious?"

"Then come with me, Gia."

I looked at him like he was crazy. "I can't come with you! I can't just up and leave. Like you just said, we aren't even in a relationship."

"Then why are you crying?"

"Fuck you," left my lips before I knew it.

He wasn't worth the explanation. He wasn't worth my tears. Come to find out, he wasn't even worth me letting my guard down, and he definitely wasn't worth Rae.

I stood from the table and walked away. I kinda wanted him to follow me. I kinda wanted him to profess his love for me, despite me knowing that there was no real love between us. I just needed to hear something that justified how I had stupidly let a piece of dick sway me into the same trap of a disloyal lying ass nigga.

Omari

It was almost four in the morning. I was riding down the e-way towards Simone's crib. My cell phone rang. It was a number that I didn't recognize, nor was it saved in my contacts.

"Hello?"

"Whad up, nephew?"

I almost veered off of the road. I fought to keep control of my Challenger, to keep it from swaying over to the shoulder of the expressway.

I had been looking for this nigga for weeks. But just like I assumed, he wasn't going to let me get away with this shit for long.

Before I could say anything, he told me, "Come holla at me."

Though he was coming at me like a man, I figured that this might be a set up. Yet, I still salivated at the thought of putting him in the same ground that he put Aeysha in, so I complied without a second thought.

"Where you at?"

He was parked in front this abandoned building on 63rd and Carpenter. At four in the morning and with it being barely twenty degrees outside, the streets were completely dark and completely quiet. As I crawled down the block, I saw Ching's Range Rover running just where he said it would be. Smoke spilled out of the exhaust as I pulled up behind it. Something told me that I should shoot Capone a text message, but I decided against it. This was between me and Ching, so there was no need in continuing to bring anybody else into it.

I still watched my back though. I grabbed my pistol from underneath my seat and held it tightly with my finger on the trigger. The metal was cold against my skin. I looked through the windows of the Range Rover and saw that Ching was the only one inside.

I could hear the locks popping just as I reached the passenger side of the vehicle. I opened the door cautiously; expecting for gunfire to meet me. Yet, Ching was simply sitting in the seat rolling a blunt. I could hear Jay Z's voice faintly.

Once I slipped into the passenger seat, he noticed the gun that I was holding, he noticed how my finger was still on the trigger, and he chuckled. "Are you serious, man?"

"I told you months ago that it was a bullet

waiting on yo' ass on this side if you ever got out."

My nerve and bravery took him by surprise. "You know, I was hoping that you was just going through some fucked up shit because of what happened to Aeysha. Your mother told my mother that you been pretty fucked up behind her murder. That's why I let you get away with this bullshit you been pullin'…"

"You ain't let me get away with shit. You shot up my spot."

"No, my block boys shot up your spot. You shot one of them. You think they was gone let you get away with that shit?"

"Just like I ain't lettin' you get away with killing Aeysha."

"I didn't kill Aeysha."

"Yes, you did."

"Nephew…"

"Stop calling me that shit!" I aimed the gun at his head before I knew it. The barrel of my pistol hit his temple so hard that it slightly knocked his head into the window.

To my surprise, he didn't react. He didn't move. He didn't retaliate. He just sat in the driver's seat, motionless, while I held the pistol against his dome.

"I'm not your fucking nephew, motherfucka! I'm not your family! Family don't do what the fuck you did! You killed her!"

He had the balls to turn towards me. The gun was pointing right between his eyes.

"If I was bogus enough to kill her, don't you think that you would be dead by now? You've stolen over a quarter million dollars worth of dope from me. You've made me look like a punk ass nigga to my entire camp because I ain't popped yo' ass."

I didn't try to stop my tears from falling. It hurt me to the point of great sadness that I was about to blow the brains out of a man that I looked up to for all of my life, a man that ended up hurting me in a way that I will never get over.

At the same time, it brought such tears of joy that I was finally about to show Aeysha that I was the man that I always wanted to be for her, protecting her with all of my ability.

Simone

When I woke up the next morning, it caught me off guard that Omari wasn't there. He sent me a text message during the middle of the night saying that he was still at the spot but would be home shortly. I was so sleepy that I didn't even respond.

Before going to shower for work, I called him a few times, but didn't get an answer. I figured that he'd gotten too drunk to drive and decided to spend the night at one of the spots. That had happened a few times in the past. I was actually appreciative that he wasn't home. I didn't have to force myself to regurgitate like I usually did while in the bathroom in the morning.

I hated throwing up. I hated those fucking prenatal pills. And I definitely hated how fat I was letting myself get.

Yet, it would all be over soon. As I dressed for work, I imagined how beautiful Erica's baby would be. I gloated in the thought of Omari and I bathing our baby boy for the first time. I relished in the joy of me and Omari's family finally being complete. I was tickled pink how in the same instance, I would be destroying the happily ever after that Tre played me for.

    I called Omari's phone a few more times as I gathered my purse and keys. Again, I didn't get an answer. I sent him a text message asking him to call me as soon as he woke up to let me know that he was okay. I thought that maybe I should drive by the spots just to make sure that he was there. My natural female insecurities began to surface. When I met Omari, he'd had a woman for years and yet fucked me relentlessly with no problem. I got sick with worry, wondering if he had gone back to his old ways and that I was starting to reap what I sowed.

    I was so wrapped up in my thoughts as I left out of the condo that I had no idea that someone was standing on the other side of the front door until he was so close that his large stature overshadowed me. At first I was relieved, assuming that the man was Omari. But when I recognized who he really was, my relief turned into panic.

    When our eyes met, my heart fell to the deepest pit of my stomach and I became weak with pure terror. Chills that felt like death feverishly ran down my spine. As he charged towards me, I was suddenly extremely sorrowful for everything that I had done. For the first time, I was sorry for killing Aeysha. I was especially remorseful for smothering that poor baby to death. I condemned myself over and over again.

I attempted to fight back as he grabbed me around my neck, but he was so powerful as he attacked me that I could feel my acrylic nails ripping away from my fingertips as my hands collided with his attack.

I clawed at his hand around my neck while trying desperately to breathe, hoping that someone would come out of their home and see our confrontation.

"No! Stop!" I tried to scream, but his hand was so tight around my throat that I could barely get out the words. "Jimmy, no!"

Chance

I was leaving that morning. By the time Capone and Omari woke up and did their rounds at the spots, I would be on a flight to Georgia.

"I just came to get my things."

Gia stood in her doorway with annoyance all over her face. I hadn't seen her since she walked out on me earlier that morning at the restaurant. I hadn't followed her once she stormed out. I simply sat at the table in White Palace trying to figure out a way to get around leaving Chicago. I didn't want to leave, and seeing Gia's reaction made me want to stay even more.

But even though I wracked my brain, it was evident that I didn't have a choice but to get on the flight. So, about thirty minutes ago, I finally left the restaurant.

Proof of Gia's pain was all over her face. Her makeup was smeared. Her hair was all over her head. I knew that she hadn't been to sleep.

She reluctantly moved out of the way to let me in. I promised myself to make this quick. I only had a few things in her room that I needed to grab; clothes, shoes, hats, and a stash of cash in her drawer.

I wanted to make it quick because I knew that I was hurting her. I knew that my distance and dry attitude towards leaving was making her regret every moment she had spent with me. But there was no way that I could explain this shit to her. It was for her own good that I just bounced without telling her anything.

I didn't want to leave her. I would have given anything to stay in the Chi, fucking her and working alongside Omari and Capone, but that shit was too risky. It was time for me to bounce. I convinced myself that I could create a similar life in Georgia.

"Gia..."

I wanted to apologize. She sat on the couch with tears in her eyes. I knew that leaving wasn't what was pissing her off. It was the fact that on top of Rae killing herself damn near in front of her, I was pulling this move. She was pissed at my nerve. She was pissed at me for not living up to my bargain of being real.

I couldn't blame her.

She cut off my apology by cutting her eyes at me. I sighed heavily, deciding not to say anything and just bounce. I rested my keys and phone on the coffee table and disappeared into her bedroom a few feet away.

I felt like shit for so many reasons. Gia and I talked about her trust issues with men for hours. When we first met, she told me so many stories of niggas fucking her over to the point that she was open to Rae's affectionate, loving, and trusting lesbian relationship.

I hated to be another man on her list that hurt her. I wasn't in love with her, but I cared for her and was looking forward to the day that we made the commitment to be together forever. I wanted her to know that I was leaving against my own will and that I would do anything to change the things that I'd done in my past that made it impossible for me to stay in Chicago.

Leaving was something that I had to do. She wouldn't understand but, by the way my life was going, I figured she was better off without me anyway.

"Who the fuck is Simone?!"

Gia's shouts caught me off guard as I was throwing my clothes into a duffle bag. I spun around, looking at her like she was crazy. That's when my keys, which were once flying through the air, smacked me dead in the nose.

"'Why did you do this to me?' 'You were supposed to be with me'!"

I held my face as I picked up my keys from the floor. All the while, the words that Gia was quoting sounded so eerily familiar. I recognized them as text messages that I had been sending to Simone in frustration. My heart sank, realizing what Gia thought she'd read.

"You lying son of a bitch!"

Then she threw my phone across the room. I was able to catch it before it hit me in the face as well.

Gia continuously screamed as tears streamed down her face. "Get the fuck out!! NOW! GET THE FUCK OUT!!"

OMARI

I was flying down the expressway when Capone finally called me back.

I hurriedly turned down Chief Keef and answered the phone with, "Meet me at my crib."

"What? Nigga, its seven o'clock in the morning."

"You don't sound sleep."

Capone laughed slyly. "Nah, I wasn't."

Then I heard some little cute girlish giggle so close that it sounded like she was on three-way with us.

"Get out the pussy and meet me at the condo. It's been a hell of a morning."

"Word?"

"Word."

"See you in a minute."

"One."

Since Capone had got a spot not too far from Simone's, I knew that he would be there within minutes, just as I was.

As soon as I hung up, I called Simone's cell again. Again, I didn't get an answer. She left for work at seven o'clock every day, so I knew that she wasn't sleep. I was sure that she was probably pissed that I was out all night and hadn't been answering her calls.

I knew she thought that I was in some pussy all night.

I blew her phone up all the way to the crib, all while trying to wrap my head around how things went down with Ching.

Capone was pulling up in front of my crib at the same time I was.

As soon as he got out of the car, he was barking at me with eyes that were riding low and hazy. "Man, what the fuck is going on?"

"I got some shit to tell you. C'mon, let's go in the crib."

I was busy dialing Simone's cell again as Capone asked me over and over again what the fuck was going on. But now I was more so worried about Simone then telling him about what went down earlier that morning. Simone had never gotten so upset with me that she ignored my calls. With her being pregnant, I was especially worried.

Still, Capone was all over me, wondering what the emergency was. As I unlocked the door, he nagged me over and over again. I'm sure he noticed how wired I was and how whatever happened had me freaking out. "Man, what the fuck is…"

As I opened the door, Capone stopped dead in his tracks.

"Oh shit," slipped from my mouth as my eyes fell on Simone lying on the kitchen floor, unconscious.

"Fuck!" Full of panic and dread, I ran towards her as fast I could. "Call 9–1–1!"

GIA

I was so mad! Though Chance had left out of my home with his tail between his legs, it wasn't enough. I drove at record speeds in pure shock at what I'd read in his phone.

I felt like I was being Catfished. I just knew that at any moment, Ashton Kutcher was going to jump out from behind a tree with a camera crew and tell me that I was being punk'd.

The level of Chance's deceit sickened me literally. I saw myself trusting him, cooking for him, sucking his dick, and fucking him, and fought the urge to scream in anger as I drove down 79th Street. These niggas talk you into putting your guard down with no intent but to shit on you and fuck up your life with no mercy.

I took care of that son of a bitch. I gave him somewhere to lay his head when all he had was that filthy ass motel to sleep in. I cooked him meals when he didn't even have a fucking dollar to buy a double cheeseburger off the dollar menu at McDonald's.

Rae killed herself. Rae was dead all because I was too far up in this lying niggas ass to make sure that she was okay.

All of that for this; a nigga who was completely opposite of what he showed me. He wooed me while lying to me. He manipulated the fuck outta me while holding me and calling me his wife.

I wasn't going to let him get away with it. He was the first nigga to fuck me over in a long time, but I was going to be the first bitch that fucked him over.

I parked sloppily, hopped out of the car, and literally ran towards the door. People looked at me like I was crazy. They saw my tears. They saw my hair sticking up every which way all over my head. They saw the distress in my eyes and watched me curiously; wondering what my problem was.

My problem was that I had stupidly trusted again. I had been laying up with a man that I had just found out was not only a liar but a monster.

"Yes, ma'am? Can I help you?" The officer at the front desk gave me the same peculiar stares that everyone in the precinct parking lot had. But I wasn't trying to hide my distress. I didn't give a fuck. Chance was going to pay for fucking me over.

"I need to speak to a homicide detective," I said

nearly out of breath with a voice cracking with anxiety and hurt. "I have information about a murder."

Secrets of a Side Bitch 3

Written By Jessica N. Watkins

Chapter One

Simone

"Okay, Miss Campbell. We'll get out of your hair now and let you rest. If you think of anything else, please give me a call."

I simply nodded my head. Omari took the card that the officer was handing us. Then the Latino officer met his partner at the door of the hospital room and left.

"How are you feeling?"

This was the first time that Omari had been able to see me since the ambulance picked me up from the condo. I became conscious again to sounds of sirens and the blurry vision of a young EMT putting an IV in my arm.

Once at the hospital, as doctors examined me to gauge the extent of my injuries, police officers asked me a series of questions that I dared not answer honestly. I couldn't tell them that Jimmy was the one that attempted to choke the life out of me.

The entire time that he kicked my ass, he blamed me for Tammy's death. He told me how he saw me at Tammy's mother's house the night that she was killed. As always, he was stalking Tammy that night. He saw me come over to her mother's house and he saw when I left. Therefore, he knew that I was the one that killed her and had since been stalking me, waiting on his opportunity to seek his revenge.

I guess it didn't matter to him that he'd spent months stalking her to do the same.

Luckily, Jimmy was so fucking psycho that he couldn't murder correctly. I did the same thing that Tammy told me that she did when he shot her; played dead. Unfortunately, he continued to choke me until my mental lights went out and I lost consciousness. Luckily, he thought I was dead and left.

I couldn't tell the police about Jimmy. Through mutual friends of Tammy's, I knew that there was a warrant out for Jimmy's arrest for his initial attempted murder charge for trying to shoot Tammy and her actual murder.

If they found Jimmy, he would be able to tell them that I was the one that killed Tammy, so I lied to the officers and told them that it was a crack head who robbed me for imaginary cash that was missing from my Louis Vuitton.

They questioned me for hours between tests and x-rays. Three cracked ribs and a bruised neck later, Omari was finally able to see me.

"I don't feel anything," I said with a slightly intoxicated giggle as I tapped the morphine drip.

"They're giving you morphine? What about the baby?"

Since I was so damn high, it took me a few seconds to register the meaning of his question. Once it registered, it took me a moment to come up with a legitimate answer.

The nurse inquisitively looked between Omari and I.

Nervously, I told him, "I lost the baby, Omari."

I could hear Omari sigh in disappointment, but my eyes were on the nurse. I wanted her to catch my hint, for her to shut the fuck up, because I knew that she would know from my charts that I really wasn't pregnant.

Yet, she kept her head low as she changed my IV.

"Damn," Omari cursed.

"I'm so sorry, baby."

"Why are you sorry?"

"I'm tired of you suffering. You've lost so much. I really felt terrible when they told me that I lost him. I was sad, but more than anything, I was sad that you had to suffer another loss."

I could see from the corner of my eye that the nurse was grimacing.

Omari shushed me by kissing me gently and quickly on the lips and rubbing my forehead.

Eboni

"Oh shiiiiiiiiiit!"

Deep breaths weren't helping me. The annoying ass cold towel that my mama kept putting on my forehead wasn't helping either, so I slapped her hand away.

"Aaaaaaaargh!"

I thought that since I'd done this three times already, that the fourth time would be a breeze, a walk in the park.

But fuck that. This shit hurt!

"Breathe," my mother told me as she stood closely next to me in the hospital bed. "Just breathe, baby."

"Mama, it's a damn baby coming out of me! Breathing ain't workin'!"

As soon as I heard the nurse snicker, I cut my eyes at her. I knew I looked crazy. I'd gone into labor at three o'clock that morning. The purple silk bonnet holding my weave was cocked to the side. Four bundles and twenty-two inches of Brazilian hair were trying to fall out of the bonnet as my head rocked back and forth in pure-all-out agony. It had been eight hours. Yet, I was only eight centimeters dilated. My contractions were the worst. It felt like this baby was trying to come out of my back!

"Whew! Oh my God." I lay back and was finally able to relax as the umpteenth contraction finally went away.

"Mama," I said breathless as I watched the nurse walk out. "I want another nurse."

"Why?"

"She's trying to kill me. She thinks this shit is funny. Why is she taking so long with the epidural?"

My mom had the nerve to laugh. "You said you didn't want it."

"That was three centimeters ago! I changed my mind. Mama, please tell them to give me the epidural."

She patted my leg like that damn pat was going to soothe me. "Okay, baby."

After Aeysha's death, I never played with death. I never said anything regarding dying and anyone. But at the moment, I swear, I just wanted to die. God could have taken me right then because the pain was just too much to bear.

He was punishing me. I know He was.

"Oh God!" I sat up and held on tightly to the bed rails to brace myself. "Mama, here comes another one!"

I grabbed her hand. For that split second, I forgot that she was my sixty year old mother, because I squeezed her hand with all of my might. "Aaaaaarggh!!!"

CHANCE

"What up, Chance?"

I tried to act as nonchalant as possible as I walked towards Fred, who was at the front door of the spot in Riverdale.

I shook up with him. "What up, boy?"

"What it do? What you doin' here?"

"Lost my phone. You seen it?"

"Nah. But I ain't been here that long."

"Paula in there?"

"Nah. Her hype ass probably took it."

I laughed, trying to hide my nervousness. "She wouldn't do that. Let me go in there and try to find it."

Even though I knew the house was empty and that Fred wouldn't miss money by leaving his post, I was nervous as shit as I walked through the spot. I didn't want anyone to come in and catch me.

When I got to the pantry where I knew the bricks were stashed in the floorboard, I took my book bag off my back. Quickly, I took the three bricks that Simone had stolen and given to me. It took me seconds to go into the pantry and return the stolen bricks back to their stash spot amongst countless other bricks in the floor board.

Fuck Simone.

I wasn't about to let that bitch run my life no more. I was two blocks away from the airport when I realized what the fuck I was doing. I wasn't letting that bitch win.

Fuck that.

So I got back on the expressway and came to the spot to return the bricks. That way, I could live in this city without looking over my shoulder. And I could still get money at the spot under Omari and Capone.

I felt bad for my involvement in killing Omari's girl. If I could take it back, I would. But that was in the past. I was ready to get on with my life with Gia and making money with my fam.

Simone was going to have to deal with it.

"Aye, man."

Fred scared the fuck outta me. Even though I was out of the pantry and putting my book bag back on my back by then, my current state of mind just had me shook.

"You heard about Omari's girl?"

Again, my heart started beating fast as fuck. But I stayed cool on the outside. "Nah. What about her?"

"Capone called me earlier. Talking about somebody robbed her. Beat her up real bad. They found her unconscious at her crib this morning."

"Word? Damn. That's fucked up," was all I cared to say.

I couldn't even feel bad for her psycho ass. I actually wished that whoever it was that had robbed her would have murked her crazy ass. Who I did feel bad for was Omari. Homeboy had gone through a lot on account of that bitch. My gut told me that Simone had something to do with Dahlia's death too.

Death just surrounded Simone. That chick was the spirit of Death itself.

I shook the eerie feeling as I made my way out of the spot. "I found my phone, man. I'm out. I'll holla at you, bro."

"Ah ight, bro. Holla."

Making my way to my ride, I felt ten pounds lighter though. Moving and flipping those bricks would have been a great start, but I would have had to live the rest of my life in hiding. That was no way to live. Sure it was a possibility that the truth could come out about Aeysha's murder, but I was going to live life my way until, God forbid, it did.

I was the happiest I felt in a minute. I was ready to live my life and suffer the consequences if necessary. I felt like staying in Chicago and returning those bricks were the first adult and rational decisions that I had made in my whole entire life.

But as soon as I got to Gia's crib, I realized that maybe missing that flight was the biggest mistake of my life.

"YOU FUCKIN' MURDERER!!!"

Gia yelled at the top her lungs as soon as I used the key that she'd given me to come in. I knew that when she saw me, she wouldn't be happy. I figured that I would have to use a good explanation for leaving in the first place and who Simone was.

This shit here caught me completely off guard though! She

was backing up like she was scared of me. The closer I walked towards her, the further she damn near ran down the hall, screaming and crying.

"Get the fuck out before I call the cops!!"

"Chill, Gia." I was practically begging as I approached her with open arms.

But she wasn't hearing me.

She was literally shaking as she picked up her phone. "I'm calling the police!"

I didn't want to scare her further by making any sudden movements, but I had to. I raced towards her. Since her hands were uneasy and shaking, I easily snatched the Galaxy out of her hand.

Something had her spooked, but my presence had her curious. It was like she wanted to look at me, but she was fighting it.

"What the fuck is wrong with you, man?"

"No, what the fuck is wrong with *you*?! I saw those messages in your phone."

"I can explain who Simone is."

"Fuck that! Explain to me who the fuck Aeysha is!"

As soon as I heard her name, my instinct was to run, so I did. I bolted out of the room, but Gia was on my heels.

"Wait, Chance!" She was holding me by the hem of my shirt. "Don't leave. Please!"

I stopped because I really didn't want to go. But I couldn't turn around and face her because I didn't want her to see the tears pooling in my eyes.

Without even looking at her, I walked somberly into the living room and sat on the couch. She let me go and followed me. My head was heavy, down to the floor, as Gia slowly approached me. She sat beside me. I could feel that her heart was just as heavy as mine was.

"I killed her."

I had to tell her. She needed to know. I needed to tell somebody. I figured, maybe it would stop eating me up if I confessed. I figured, maybe if I told her, she would be the one person in my life to have my back and help me through this shit.

I still couldn't look her in the eyes. But after I said those words, she didn't move a muscle. I couldn't even hear her breathing.

"I fucked up," I said as the tears once pooling in my eyes rolled down my cheeks. "I was in the group home with no family and no friends. I had a lil' crush on this lady named Simone that worked there. She was like the only person that gave a fuck about me, ya' know? I was turning eighteen, so I had to move to transitional housing. I felt so alone, so lost, man. That and I didn't have a dollar to my name. I didn't know where my next meal was going to come from. Then Simone told me that this chick was fucking with her brother. Supposedly, she was giving Simone's brother all sorts of legal problems with their divorce and abusing their daughter. She offered me twenty-five stacks to kill her... So I did."

Still, Gia didn't move. The house was still and quiet as death, except for the sounds of her sobbing.

"I took the money and moved to Minnesota. Simone told me that she loved me and was going to move out there with me. I bought some bricks to flip, but the nigga I was living with stole them. I was popped, so I had to come back to Chicago. When I got back, I realized that Simone played me. She wasn't even trying to help me. I was broke. That's why I was staying at the motel when you met me. I kept calling her for help, but she wouldn't even answer the phone. Then one day, I bumped into one of my homeboys from school. He let me start selling work for him and his partner. Lo and behold, his partner is Simone's boyfriend. I go to his crib, and here this bitch is living the life of luxury. I put two and two together and figure out that it was Omari's girlfriend that I killed. Simone had lied to me. She had me kill that girl to get her out the way so that she could have that nigga. I just know it. Then she stole three bricks from him and gave them to me as an incentive to leave the state. She didn't want me around for the dots to connect. But I couldn't leave. I didn't want to leave what finally felt like a life. I didn't want to leave people who finally felt like family. So this morning, instead of taking that flight, I took the three bricks back and came here."

Gia burst into uncontrollable tears. She was sobbing and saying, "Oh my God."

"I know. It's fucked up. I know," was I could say.

"No, no," she cried. "I fucked up. I was so mad at you. All I saw was that you killed somebody and was threatening Simone in your text messages. I thought you were a monster."

"I'm not though, babe. I know it seems like it. But at the time, I didn't see another way…"

"Chance, I went to the police!"

My eyes shot daggers of disbelief at her. She avoided my eyes by burying her face into the pillow and crying hysterically.

"What did you tell police?!"

In response, she kept crying, kept saying "Oh my God" over and over again.

"Gia! Calm down and just talk to me, baby. What did you tell the police?"

Full of sorrow, she lifted her head from the pillow. She looked like a train wreck. She'd cried her false lashes completely off. Her eyes were swollen from crying so much.

She still couldn't look at me as she tried to explain. "I talked to a homicide detective. I told them that I went through my boyfriend's phone and saw some text messages between him and some chick, Simone, about a murder."

With each word, I felt myself dying. With every word she said, I felt my life slipping away.

"OH MY GOD!"

"But I gave them the fake name that was on your ID! Once I said all of that, I just couldn't tell on you. I couldn't do it. So I gave them the fake name."

I covered my face with my hands and tried to think. I hadn't used that particular phone for any reason but to contact Simone. I had used the phone to text message Gia a few times when we first met. I stopped as soon as I got my money up and was able to purchase a real phone.

It was a throw away that luckily couldn't be traced back to me since I always got the minutes in cash. Simone purchased it herself. But I knew that after some time, the police would be able to retrieve the text messages, if they had the phone number.

"Did you give them any other information?"

Reluctantly, she answered, "Your phone number."

"Shit!"

Instantly, Gia was clinging to me. She threw her arms around me. Her tears fell on my face. She continued to cry hysterically as she said, "I'm sorry. I'm so sorry. I was just so mad, Chance, but I didn't mean to hurt you. I'm sorry."

I hugged her back.

She needed it.

I needed it.

"Shhhh. I'm sorry too, baby. I'm sorry for hurting you. I just didn't know what else to do."

Both of us were a wreck as we sat there rocking, crying and holding each other. We were both fucked up. We were both damaged goods that had a hand in damaging each other further. But I could tell in that embrace that we both fucked with each other. There was loyalty in that embrace.

"It's going to be okay. I'll figure it out," I told her. "It's going to be okay."

Omari

I had been at the hospital all day. They were keeping Simone for observation, so I stepped out to go handle some things at the spots.

Honestly, I needed some fresh air. After Aeysha's death, that hospital smell made me sick.

"Excuse me! Excuse me, young man!"

I turned in the middle of the parking lot, wondering if the voice was calling for me. I turned to see an older woman. I noticed that it was Simone's nurse. Her shift had ended just a few minutes before I left.

She approached me cautiously.

"Hi, Nurse Jackson. Everything okay with Simone?"

"Yes, baby, everything is all right... I guess."

I could see in her eyes that something was bothering her. That put me on edge. Though I had just left Simone's bedside and she was fine, it was apparent that something was wrong.

"I really shouldn't be telling you this. It's a HIPAA violation and I can definitely lose my job. But you looked so sad, so I feel like you should know the truth."

This lady was rambling. I just wanted her to get on with it. The last two days had been long as hell. I just wanted to get to a bar and get my hands wrapped around a stiff drink.

"She wasn't pregnant, baby."

"Excuse me?"

Tenderly, she put on her hand on my shoulder. "She lied to you. She didn't lose a baby in the attack. She wasn't pregnant when she got to the hospital. We ran a pregnancy test. It's procedure with female victims."

I didn't know what to think, so I just kept looking at this lady like she was crazy. I knew she couldn't have been lying though. She had no reason to lie, and her eyes looked so sincere with genuine concern for me.

I thanked her for her honesty and promised her that I wouldn't say anything that would cause her to lose her job.

Then I walked towards my car, slowly. Suddenly, I was lost. The drama of the past two days had taken effect. I couldn't wrap my head around what the fuck was going on. I thought of the mornings Simone spent throwing up, how big her stomach had gotten, and the ultrasound of our baby boy that she'd shown me. I couldn't imagine her lying about being pregnant, but something in that nurse's eyes told me that she wasn't lying either.

Folk's eyes had been speaking to me all day. Earlier that morning, when I was pointing that gun at Ching, it's like God spoke to me. God told me to look into Ching's eyes and see the sincerity and compassion in a man's eyes that had never held such emotions.

I knew then that he had nothing to do with Aeysha's murder. I knew that he felt sorry for me when, after putting metal to his brain, he let me live. I broke down in tears, because after all this time, I was still at a loss when it came to who killed Aeysha and why. When Ching promised to help me kill the motherfucker when we found out, my tears flowed heavier than they ever had.

I promised to pay him back for every brick that I stole from him.

It was only because we were family, only because of our mothers' blood, that he let me live with that alone.

Chapter Two

Eboni

Three days later, I was in the house with three off the chain kids and a screaming newborn.

"Tati, sit down!"

Tatiana was my three-year-old.

"Lil' T, stop chasing your sister!"

Terrance, Lil' T, was six.

"And both of you be quiet before you wake up Tasia."

Tasia was two.

As I attempted to rock my newborn in one hand while waiting for his bottle to cool in the other, I cursed myself for having yet another baby.

Having another baby was an absolute ridiculous decision to make. But Aeysha's death showed me how precious life was. After seeing Aeysha dead with my own eyes, I could never take another life, so I was forced to add another kid to my lineup.

If the crying, running, and jumping wasn't enough to threaten to wake Tasia up, somebody rang my damn doorbell.

"If this is those bad ass kids from upstairs, I swear to God."

I know my kids were energetic, but that bitch upstairs was straight up raising two devils. They were eleven and nine years old, but had the mouths of grown ass men. They had told me on many occasions that I had a phat ass.

They would be in jail by their teens, I was sure.

I opened my front door and peeked out into the hallway towards the security door. I didn't see those bad ass boys on the other side of the security door. I saw the figure of a woman, but couldn't tell who it was.

"Who is it?"

"Detective Howard. I'm here to see Eboni Hawkins."

"About?"

"Aeysha Walker."

I quickly buzzed her in and stepped inside of my apartment, behind the door.

Off site, Detective Howard looked like an everyday woman, wearing a ponytail, plain black fitted tee, straight legged jeans, and gym shoes. The gun in plain sight on her hip was what verified that she was a cop. She flashed me her badge anyway before I let her in.

Lil' T and Tati looked at her curiously, but continued to play in the middle of the floor. There was no use in me making them leave the room. They were just going to find a reason to come back in anyway.

"You can have a seat," I told the detective as I moved a few toys out of the way to make room on the leather sofa.

"That is a gorgeous baby. How old is he?"

"Only three days old."

She gave him a loving smile. I know most people said that their babies were beautiful, but my baby really was. He was a splitting image of his daddy.

"You have some questions about Aeysha?"

I was use to police coming by every now and then to ask about Aeysha's murder, though the visits slowed down as time passed. Since I was the one that found her body and called 9-1-1, I was really the only witness that had any information.

But this was a new detective, so I was anxious to find out what was going on.

"Well, like I said, my name is Detective Howard. I have a few questions about Aeysha's murder. I was assigned the case a few days ago, after we received a tip."

"A tip?" That was a first, so I went from curious to excited.

"Yes. I can't really give you too much information, because we are still collecting evidence. I know you've told this story a million times. I've read the reports. But in your own words, can you tell me what happened that day?"

My heart sank just thinking about it. The deathlike feeling of watching life leave somebody's body came over me like a blanket. I tried every day to forget the vision of the blood leaking out of the holes in Aeysha's head and chest. No matter how much I tried, the vision haunted me daily.

"I had just come home from dropping my kids off at my mother's. I had gone to the grocery store to pick up a few things. I was carrying the bags in the house when I heard my phone ringing. I went in the house, dropped the bags in the kitchen, and checked my phone. It was Aeysha. I told myself to just take my coat off and run upstairs to see what was up. But I had to use the bathroom first. While in the bathroom, I heard somebody on the stairs in the hallway. I figured it was Omari, since Aeysha was on strict bed rest. Then, seconds later, I heard shots. You know, gun shots ain't all that rare out here, so I thought nothing much of it. After leaving the bathroom, I glanced outside the window real quick and didn't see any action, so I went upstairs to check on Aeysha. Her front door was open, but she wasn't in the house. And that's when it hit me that it might have been her that was on the steps. So I ran back down the stairs to get my cell to see what the hell she was doing on her feet and outside. Then, something told me to go outside and see if she had left in her car. I saw her car…," I tried hard to fight the tears so that I could continue without sounding like a crying idiot. "Then I... I saw her feet lying beside her car. I ran outside. I ran to her. It was so much blood on the pavement…"

Detective Howard put her hand on my knee to stop me. "Did you see anyone?"

"No. Nobody was outside."

"Did you see any strange vehicles?"

"No," I answered, trying hard to fight my tears.

"Are you familiar with the name Reginald Barner?"

Then Detective Howard took a piece of paper from the folder that she was holding. "I want you to look at these photos and tell me if you see anyone that you recognize.

The photo array was of women, which I found odd. But what was most peculiar was the photo of Omari's girlfriend that I recognized.

I pointed frantically at her photo. "That's Simone!"

"So you know her?"

"Yes, Omari just introduced me to her!"

"So they're dating?"

"Yes!"

Detective took out a pen and pad from her pocket and began taking notes.

"Did she have something to do with Aeysha's murder?!"

"We're just tying up some loose ends," was her generic response.

"I *told* Omari!"

Detective Howards eyebrows narrowed in suspicion. "You told Omari what?"

"I saw that bitch... Sorry... I saw *Simone* before."

"Where?"

"One day, me and Aeysha went to Leona's. This chick sits next to use at the bar and starts a conversation with us. She told us that she was a hiring manager. She didn't say that her name was Simone though. She gave us another name that I can't recall. Anyway, she even took Aeysha's number, telling her that she would call her with some job leads."

"And you told Omari this?"

"Yes! When he introduced me to her as his girlfriend. I couldn't put my finger on it right then, but once I got home it hit me. I tried to call him. I even text messaged him, but he never got back to me. I haven't heard from him since."

Detective Howard simply continued to write notes, but my head was spinning. The possibilities of why Simone and Omari would be together now and why this detective would be showing me her photo was sickening. Just the thought of these connections made me tear up.

I could have lived with Aeysha being a random victim of gun violence. Innocent people died in the city every day. It was out of control. There was nothing anyone could do to escape it but pray.

But if Aeysha was an intentional target and died by the hands of people she knew, this shit was going to be so fucked up.

"Have you seen a silver Camaro in the neighborhood before? It would look like this."

Detective Howard showed me a stock photo of what the car would look like and I froze.

I was breathless as I gasped. "Oh my God! Oh my God!"

I tried to hide how upset I was from the kids. I tried my best to hush my hysterics.

"I've seen that car on the block before! It just started appearing one day. I never saw who was in it. It was just sitting or sometimes cruising by. I thought maybe it belonged to somebody who lived on the block."

"Did you see it the day of the murder?"

I tried hard to remember. I tried *so* hard.

I was devastated when I couldn't remember, so devastated that I started to cry. "I don't know!"

Of course, Tati and Lil' T looked curiously at my tears.

Quickly, Detective Howard tried to calm me down. She even took my baby from me. Now that my hands were free, I wiped my tears from my face and hugged myself, wrapping my arms around my stomach, trying to make the pain go away.

"You have to calm down. You just had this baby. We can't have you all upset. Your body is still healing." Then, despite the intensity of the conversation that we were having, Detective Howard lost herself in my baby's face. "He is just gorgeous. What color are his eyes?"

"Gray."

SIMONE

That day, I was finally released from the hospital.

Oddly, I hadn't seen much of Omari since I was admitted. He was always running errands or taking care of business. When he did visit me, he was extremely quiet. I didn't question his distance though. I appreciated it. I didn't need him in the hospital all in my face. It was so hard for me to cover up not being pregnant and why I was assaulted.

Omari was quiet as we rode to the condo. I was caught up in my own thoughts as well. Jimmy's words were playing over and over again in my head. He hadn't killed me, but I knew his stalker potential. I knew that, once he learned that I was alive, he wouldn't stop until he found me.

Once we reached the condo, I just wanted to take a long, hot bath. I walked around, too involved in my own thoughts to pay attention to Omari's silence. I gathered fresh lounging pajamas and went into the bathroom to soak in my own thoughts.

I let nothing but hot water fill the tub. I wanted it to run all the way to the top so that the hot water could soothe my whole body. Besides the aches and pains of my injuries, my insides were aching. Things had become way too much. I was stressed and full of anxiety. Eerie chills flooded my body every time I thought of the police questioning me. Even though it was questions about my attack, and nothing about Aeysha, it still scared me to death. Just the presence of the police made me realize how real things could get.

Luckily for me, Chance was gone. As long as he stayed away, I figured I should be fine.

Omari jolted me out my deep thoughts as he entered the bathroom. To avoid the fucked up mood that he was in, I stood up from the toilet and began to undress.

"Shouldn't you be bleeding?"

Omari's question caught me so off guard that all I could reply with was, "What?"

As I picked up the pants and panties that I'd just slipped off from the floor, he snatched them from me. He threw my pants to the floor and held my panties in the air.

"Shouldn't you be bleeding? You had a miscarriage, right?"

I couldn't even say shit. I couldn't find the words to say.

Omari looked at my apparent guilt and shook his head. "Were you ever really pregnant?"

He was so calm that it was scary. I can imagine that Omari had been through so much pain that he didn't feel it anymore. I was the person that put that pain in his life. As I stood there, I was ready to defend it all – my lies, the deceit, all of it – because I did it all for him, to have him, to be with him.

"Were you?! Tell the truth, Simone."

"Yes! Yes, I was! But…" I slumped back down on the toilet. I held my face. Real tears began to flow. I didn't want to hurt him. But

I dared not ever run the risk of losing him. "I got an abortion."

"When?"

I couldn't even look at him. I could feel him hovering over me though. I could imagine him glaring at me.

"A month ago."

"Why?!"

Finally, I looked him in his eyes, ready to do or say whatever to keep my man. "Because you didn't want it!"

"That's bullshit, Simone! You talked all that shit about wanting a baby. All you talked about was the baby, and then you just kill it? That don't make sense to me."

He wasn't yelling, nor was he threatening to leave, so I figured he believed my story.

"I was tired of coming second!" I stood up to make my defense that much more believable. The tears sealed the deal. "All I hear all fuckin' day is Aeysha this and Dahlia that. I am not apart of your life. I'm just here. I just exist. You didn't want my baby. You wanted your family!"

He couldn't argue with me. Despite my lies, I was right about him not wanting my baby. He knew that. Instead of fussing and fighting, he tried to soften the blow.

"I'm still mourning, Simone. What the fuck you want me to do? Forget about Aeysha and my baby? Never talk about them?"

"I want you stop comparing me to her. Stop expecting me to be her."

Again, he couldn't argue with me. Yet, he still held on to what I knew was the truth. "I still don't understand why you would get an abortion behind my back. No, I wasn't ecstatic about having another baby. You knew that though! But I was coming around. You know all the shit that I have been through. You've been right here, front and center, while I face loss after loss, why do this shit to me again?"

"Because I didn't want my baby coming in second to somebody else. I live with that feeling every day. I didn't want my baby to have to do the same."

OMARI

She was full of shit. I knew it.

Luckily for her, the baby was already gone. I was forced to learn months ago that I couldn't control loss. The baby was gone, but I had present things to attend to.

"Look." I ran my hand over my head in frustration. Simone continued to stand in front of me with tears rolling down her face that, no matter what, I just couldn't believe. I knew that this lie had done it for me. There she stood, half naked, and, real talk, she repulsed me. I couldn't believe that, after watching me hurt, she would purposely inflict more hurt on me.

But she felt guilty. I saw the guilt. So I fed on it.

"It is what it is. If you felt like you needed to have an abortion, it's nothing I can do about that now *obviously*."

She flinched at how dismissive I was. But I continued to talk like I didn't see her hurt, just like she continued to act like she didn't see mine. "I need a favor, though. I got something to take care of. I need some cash."

I had to pay Ching back. He promised to squash this beef along with me if I paid him back wholesale value for the work that I stole. I had some racks in savings. I knew Simone had some from selling her mom's crib. With both combined, I would be able to pay

Ching back at least half of what I owed him. I figured that would show him an act of good faith until I came up with the rest. That should have only taken me a few weeks, considering how both traps were jumping.

Just as I assumed, Simone didn't argue with me. She was real eager to help, just to get the spotlight off of her. "How much do you need?"

"How much do you have?"

"Well, I still have about twenty thousand…"

"I need that."

She was taken by surprise. "Why so much?"

"You'll have it back in a few weeks. I gotta take care of something," was all I was willing to explain. She was already ready to pop off any time I mentioned Aeysha. I couldn't tell her about my interaction with Ching and why I had to do this.

But just like always, she said okay. But unlike always, her ready eagerness made me question her motives.

Once Simone told me that she would go to the bank the next day, I let her have her privacy. Then I sent Ching a text message telling him that I had almost half of what I owed him.

I still had a lot of wonder. I wondered if this would truly settle this beef. I had broken every street code. But the fact that he let me live despite breaking those codes let me know that he didn't kill Aeysha.

I still wondered what in the hell happened to her. I hoped for it to be a case of mistaken identity or some random drive by.

Considering the hood that we lived in at the time, who knew.

Chance

"You believe that?"

Waiting for an answer, Capone was looking at Omari like he was crazy as hell. It was fucked up that I couldn't even give Omari the same look. I had to believe him. I knew first hand that he was right.

"Yea, I believe him." Omari gulped a shot of Patron. The shot glass hit the table hard. There was a lot on his mind. I could see the stress all over his face. The weariness was running over in his eyes.

Omari and Capone watched each other reluctantly. I sat there like a deer trying to avoid the headlights.

"Are you sure?" Capone's question was like a jab in my heart. It was like an outer body experience being in the middle of this conversation. "If Ching didn't kill her, who did?"

Omari's shoulders barely shrugged. The weight on them kept them from moving freely. "I don't know. Probably was a drive by, mistaken identity or some shit. We lived in the hood, man. People get shot every day. Innocent people. So ain't no tellin'."

Capone didn't know what to say. He just sat there, staring at Omari in disbelief.

"Man, dawg, I know that I look like I punked out. But he didn't kill Aeysha. I believe him."

Honestly, I was happy that Omari was falling back off Ching. No matter the things that I'd done in the past, I wasn't a bad person.

I didn't want Ching to get killed for some shit he didn't do. I especially didn't want to have to help kill him, knowing that he was dying for something that I did.

I could see in Omari's eyes that it was fucking with him not knowing who killed her, though. There was months of stress on him that was making him age before our eyes.

"I'm just going to let the police handle it."

Omari's words shook the shit outta me.

Capone smacked his lips in disbelief. "Are they even still investigating it?"

"Yea. Matter fact, I got a call from a detective earlier today. Don't know what that's about. Probably just wanna ask more questions. They do that every now and then when they are looking at the case. I'll holla at her tomorrow though."

Again, I was wondering if not getting on that plane a few days ago was a smart move.

Gia had spent the last few days sucking my dick into believing how sorry she was for running to the cops. Just like Capone couldn't believe that Omari believed Ching, a large part of me couldn't believe that I was actually standing behind Gia. It was something about her that just convinced me that behind that damaged girl was a loyal bitch that just made a mistake.

We could get it right. I could hustle this block like a motherfucker until I had enough to racks to cop my own weight legitimately. Then Gia and I could bounce to Houston, Dallas, or Cali.

We could leave and avoid any wrath that might be coming.

That was my plan. I listened to Omari convince Capone of Ching's innocence, realizing how swiftly I had to put that plan into action.

Time was running out.

Chapter Three

Simone

"Thanks."

Omari barely looked at me as he took the envelope full of money that I was handing him through the window of my car.

I was giving him my last. It was the last of my savings. I was down to a few hundred dollars left out of my paycheck. I had cleared my accounts for this nigga. Yet, he was still looking at me with regret. There was disappointment all over his face.

"What time are you going to be home?"

He shrugged his shoulders while looking down the street, avoiding my eyes. "I don't know."

The pregnancy was ten steps forward. Now I had violently fallen twenty steps back. On top of living in Aeysha's shadow, now I was suspect in his eyes.

He barely wanted to say anything to me before he walked away from my car. "I'll holla at you," was what he barely shot back over his shoulder as he walked back towards the spot.

I stared at him, wondering what I could possibly do to fix this. Watching him walk towards the house was like watching him walk out of my life. It hurt. It felt like a knife slowly slicing my heart.

As I stared disappointedly at Omari, I thought I saw Chance walk out of the house and meet Omari on the porch.

I gasped as I frantically rolled the window back down to get a better look. "What the fuck?!"

Sure enough, it was Chance! He met my gaze and looked away like he was suppose to fucking be there!

"Stupid motherfucka!" I was livid as I peeled off.

I was freaking the fuck out. He was supposed to have his ass in some country ass town in Georgia! My thoughts were racing as I sped onto the expressway. Last I heard, he was on his way to the airport. I wondered what the fuck he was doing back in Chicago. Better yet, I wondered who the fuck he thought he was to be back at the spot!

I couldn't breathe. A panic attack was approaching. I tried to calm down. I tried to tell myself not to worry about it and to handle it later. I had to handle one thing at a time. That first thing was getting Omari back on my good side. He was barely talking to me. He didn't want to look at me. He hadn't touched me since I was in the hospital.

I'd done too much and gone too far to still be losing.

I was so super stressed. I couldn't even feel the approaching summer sun surrounding me as I got out my Benz and walked towards my condo. I was so consumed in my own thoughts. I could only hear the heels of my Giuseppe pumps as they clacked against the pavement.

That is, until an unfamiliar voice called my name. "Simone? Simone Campbell?"

I foolishly turned to meet the voice, confirming that I was indeed Simone Campbell.

A light-skinned woman with a ponytail, dressy tee, and black slacks was behind me. She was leaving a parked sedan and walking towards me. I wondered who the fuck she was.

She responded to the curiosity spread all over my face. "Hi. I'm Detective Howard."

She even shook my hand, as if her visit was friendly. But my gut knew that this visit was far from friendly. It was the one thing that I'd hoped would never happen. It was the beginning of my end. It was obviously the reason why Chance felt like it was okay to stay in Chicago. Immediately, I figured that he snitched or something. Nothing, no evidence, should have led a detective to me.

"Hi," I said, shaking her hand reluctantly. "May I help you?"

I hoped that she was a narcotics detective. I hoped that she was here because Omari had gotten himself in some sort of trouble.

"Yes. I have a few questions. But can we step into your home to talk?"

She noticed how defensive my stance was. I tried my best to be nonchalant, but I couldn't help but be anxious.

"What is this about?"

Her response was repetitive. "I just have a few questions.

May I come in?"

"Do you have a warrant or something?"

Detective Howard snickered. "No, Miss Campbell, I don't."

Smiling, I answered, "Well, I would have been happy to let you in if you had one. But, since you don't, I'm more than happy to talk to you out here."

With her hands in the pockets of her blazer, she leaned against the fence surrounding the condominium. Every ounce of my being wanted to run inside of the building and hide.

Finally, she told me what her visit was about. "I have some questions about Aeysha Walker."

Immediately, my heart stopped. I fought to keep my composure. I fought to breathe freely. "Oh, well you would want to talk to Omari about that…"

"No, I have questions for *you*."

"Well, I wouldn't know anything about her murder. I wasn't really around during that time. I mean, I knew Omari, but we didn't start dating until after Aeysha's murder."

"What is your relationship with Reginald Barner?"

Instead of stopping, my heart was now beating so fast and hard that I was getting dizzy. I wondered how the fuck she knew about the fake name on the ID that I had given Chance. The possibilities of him going to the police were becoming more and more likely.

"I don't know a Reginald Barner."

"He's been texting you a lot."

Frantically, I looked up and down the street. I was buying time, trying to figure out the right reply. I was also looking out for Omari. If he was here to witness this line of questioning, he would leave me for sure.

"Look, I don't think I should be talking to you without a lawyer."

Casually, Detective Howard responded, "A lawyer isn't needed, Miss Campbell. Not at the moment anyway."

"I still prefer not to talk to you without one."

With a smirk, she told, "You're free to go. You have a good day."

She walked away as smoothly as she arrived. I eyed the gun on her hip as she walked back towards the unmarked car. I cursed myself for not noticing the car when I pulled up in the first place. Yet, I had a feeling, whether it was that day or the next, there was no way of avoiding this.

She would be back.

Eboni

"This bitch." I was literally growling under my breath as I followed the kids up the stairs. My baby was sleeping in my running truck next to the curb a few feet away.

Felicia had the nerve to hug and kiss my kids as they barged into the front door of the two-story home in the south suburbs of the city.

"Can you tell Terrance to come to the door?" I barely gave that bitch eye contact. Fuck that bitch. She was lucky I wasn't whooping her ass off sight.

I stood at the bottom of the steps, keeping my eye on my truck and the doorway.

When he finally appeared in the doorway, Terrance acted like talking to me was repulsive. "What's up?"

He was already barely taking care of my kids before. But once he found out that I was pregnant again, he was straight up treating me like a thot. At this point, I had to practically beg him to spend time with the kids. Getting financial help from him was purely through the courts. Even that was the bare minimum, because he was able to cheat the system since he was mostly paid in cash.

"Why you can't answer the phone? Why I gotta call Felicia to get through to you? You were supposed to pick the kids up today. I didn't want to have to come out the house with my baby."

Terrance stood in the doorway, looking at me like a

simpleton. "What's wrong with you calling Felicia?"

"You know damn well why I don't want to call that bitch!"

Felicia's voice could be heard immediately. "Who are you calling a bitch?!" Then she was standing next to Terrance in the doorway, looking just as frustrated and disgusted with my presence as he was.

Quickly, I forgot that one of my babies was in the truck and that the others were in the house. "I'm calling you a bitch, *bitch*!"

I missed no opportunity to curse this hoe, nor did she miss any opportunity to come at my head. Therefore, we were charging towards one another, ready to attack.

As soon as she was in arm's reach, I was swinging on that bitch. For over a year, I wanted nothing more than to tag this bitch a few good times. Every time I had to pay a bill without Terrance's help, every time my kids asked me why their daddy didn't live with us anymore, every time I couldn't buy my kids what they wanted because I didn't have that much money, I wanted to outright murder this bitch.

But, of course, Terrance found his way in between us before either one of us could connect with the other. Yet, as always, he was protecting *her* and defending *her*.

Wearing polo flip flop house shoes, socks, basketball shorts and a white tee, he pushed me away from his house.

I didn't give a fuck. I was pushing him back, refusing to leave as I spat at Felicia. "Fuck you! I'll call you whatever the fuck I wanna call you! You's a bitch and you's a hoe! You snake ass bitch!"

"Don't be mad at me cuz I won, bitch!"

I tried to go straight through Terrance. He was 6'3" and damn near three hundred pounds, but I attempted to knock him over like a feather just to get to that bitch's throat.

"Get the fuck away from my crib!" Terrance grabbed me by my shoulders and pushed me away like a disobedient puppy. The way Terrance looked at me like I was disgusting pissed me off even more.

At one point, this man loved me to death. He once loved me so much that we had three kids together. Suddenly, this bitch, Felicia, was able make him turn on me. He turned his back on everything I meant to him and his children with one whiff of the pussy.

"Fuck both of you bitches," I said as I walked away.

I heard Terrance say, "Get yo' bum ass away from my crib actin' crazy, bitch."

Now I was a bum. Just last year, he loved me, but now I was a bum.

I couldn't give him or her any more energy. I flipped him off as I climbed into my 2012 Expedition that I was able purchase with my tax return a few months ago.

I fought tears stubbornly. Months ago, I swore that I would never let Terrance or Felicia bring me to tears again.

Terrance and I had been together for ten years. I'd been the bitch that had his back in high school, when he got in fights, got suspended and got kicked out. I was the bitch that bailed him out of jail over and over again. I was the one that took my kids to countless hearings as he fought drug cases. I was the bitch that helped him clean out the barbershop that he purchased to go legit.

But my best friend since kindergarten, since the years of glue sticks and crayons, she was the bitch that started fucking him behind my back once he was the legit paid businessman that he always wanted to be. She wasn't that much prettier than me. But what she did have was education, good credit, and class. For six months, they were fucking behind my back. I had no clue until he came home, to the same apartment that I live in now, and told me that he was leaving me for her. Lo and behold, she was outside in his truck, waiting for him to get his things so that he could go home with her to the new home that he'd purchased in the suburbs in her name without me even knowing.

He'd created a new posh life for her and left me in the hood to take care of three kids. That new life didn't have much room for our kids. Terrance barely helped me financially and hardly ever spent time with the kids. It was like he had this perfect new life that didn't include his children.

I didn't know what hurt worse – their betrayal or their ability to stick the knife further in my back by treating me and our kids like low life problems.

I know it's not an excuse, but that was my only reason for

fucking Omari in the first place. It was nothing personal against Aeysha. I loved Aeysha to death. Slowly, we became real friends. Yet, my friendship with her had nothing to do with having sex with Omari. In my mind, there was absolutely no connection. He was nothing but a dog ass nigga, just like every other man. He was the same ain't shit nigga that my kids' father was. Omari was a toy. He was just something to pass the time by and to fuck with, like my baby's father was fucking with me. Omari was that thing that I used to make myself temporarily feel better, like a drink or a blunt.

    I was using Omari. He was a piece of dick.

    Aeysha deserved better.

    So did I.

Chapter Four

Simone

"Why did you get that abortion?"

Omari's voice caught me off guard. I didn't know that he was awake as I lay with my back to him. My eyes were staring at nothing in particular. My eyes were idle, but my mind was racing.

Since Detective Howard left yesterday, I had been trying to connect the dots on my own. I was trying to figure out what evidence she had that led her to me. I wondered if once she returned if I would be able to explain my way out of it. I thought of blaming it all on Chance. I thought of continuing to play innocent.

Nothing made sense.

"I know you hear me."

Omari's anger was making this worse. He was so mad at me. He no longer trusted me. One appearance from the police would have him looking at me even more suspiciously.

"I felt alone," was my answer.

"How the fuck did you feel alone? I was right here, Simone. Every day. I know that mentally I was somewhere else, but what the fuck did you expect? My girl just died. My baby just died. Anybody would be mentally fucked after that."

"You! You! You! You! It's all about you and yours! What about me?!" I was angry, but the source of that anger was making me lash out at Omari. "Do you understand what I go through being with you?!"

I stayed lying on my side. I couldn't even look at him. I was being insensitive and I knew it.

I wanted to be nicer. I wanted to be there for him. I wanted to defend myself with loving words that convinced him otherwise. Yet, I was too busy running the questions that Detective Howard asked over and over again in my mind. I ran my responses over and over in my mind, wondering if I was convincing enough.

I knew that I looked and sounded guilty.

Detective Howard's condemning smirk was embedded in my brain, telling me that she was convinced of my guilt.

I heard Omari exhale in frustration before I felt his weight leave the bed. Tears were in my eyes as I watched him leave out of the room.

The room was spinning. My mind was racing. My throat was closing due to the ball of fear stuck in the middle of it.

I tried all night to be calm. All night, I attempted to think rationally. I tried to convince myself that everything would be okay. I tried to tell myself that there was no way that the police would be able to connect me to this murder.

I was a bit irrational at times. Hell, I could admit that I was desperate at many times in my life. But I was never ever stupid.

Therefore, I knew that there was something connecting me to "Reginald Barner". Some how, some way, they had been able to miraculous find out this fake name and connect it to me. There was only a small amount of time before additional connections were made.

The doorbell rang, shooting terror through every one of my nerves. I jumped out of bed. I wanted to run and answer the door before Omari did. My hands were shaking. My limbs were uncontrollable. I just knew that it was Detective Howard back with more questions.

This was it. It was all over.

"Who is it?"

I didn't even realize that Omari was already in the kitchen and a few feet away from the door.

I stood in the middle of the bedroom floor, with one leg in a pair of shorts, frozen in immense fear.

I was breathless.

I was terrified.

The window behind me suddenly seemed like a beautiful escape.

When I heard Capone's voice, relief rushed violently through my body so aggressively that I fell onto the bed.

I couldn't continue to live that way, in that much fear.

"Simone, I'm gone. I'll be back in a minute."

Omari didn't even give me a chance to reply before I heard

the door slam shut.

The dots had begun to connect. It wouldn't take long for the police to connect me to purchasing the phone that Chance had been using. It wouldn't take long for them to retrieve the text messages and hundreds of phone calls between me and "Reginald Barner". I didn't know how they had connected the dots, but they were connected. It was time for me to run before they fully connected to me.

For months, I wouldn't leave Omari. For months, I figured out ways to keep him.

Now, it was time to run. I had to run far away from the man that I'd fought so hard for– that I'd killed for. To my heart, running was impossible. But I couldn't just stay there and wait for the police to come back when they had more evidence.

My stomach balled up in knots as I checked my account balances through the Chase app on my phone. I then realized that I'd given Omari my last dime the day before. I only had enough to survive on my own for a week. I wondered how much gas it would take to get me to the next state, but taking my car was too risky. Therefore, I knew that after purchasing a Greyhound bus ticket to wherever I chose to go, I would be broke.

My eyes landed on the closet of my bedroom and it hit me. It was possible that Omari had a stash spot somewhere in the house.

I tore up every closet, looked through every drawer, and picked at every loose floorboard. But there was nothing. There wasn't even a brick that I could attempt to sell.

I thought of going to the spots and cleaning out the stash spots, but in case I was able to weasel my way out of this, if eventually the dust settled on an unsolvable murder and I could convince Omari that the police were just targeting me, I didn't want to add fuel to the fire.

I was forced to get into my car with four hundred and thirty-two dollars and ninety cents. I wanted to pack everything, but I wasn't sure how long I would need to be gone. I wasn't sure what would make me look guilty. I packed a few essential items into a Louis Vuitton duffel bag and reluctantly left the life that my devious crimes had built.

Every minute, every second, I felt like I would see that sedan pulling up. As I started my car, my heart raced every time a car drove by and every time a car slowed down next to me.

Hesitantly, I looked back at the condo. I stopped before turning the ignition. I wondered if I could fight this. I wondered if I could continue to deny, continue to weave this web of lies, and keep my life with this man. I wondered if leaving would seal my incarcerated fate. I wondered if staying would do the same.

I didn't know what the fuck to do. But what I did know was that comfortably living in that house with Omari was no longer an option. Living daily while wondering when the next visit from that detective would be, if the next time she would have more evidence and an arrest warrant for me, was not an option. Finally, I had no choice but to let Omari go.

I started the car with a heavy heart and a fear filled mind. I wondered if what I was doing was right. As I rode through the streets of downtown, I knew that, whether it was right or wrong, staying was no longer a smart move.

Arriving at the Greyhound Station on West Harrison, I parked my car on the street and left it for good. I knew that eventually it would be towed. Entering the station, I had no idea where I was headed. I just knew that I needed to get somewhere far away, with so many people that I would blend amongst the bodies.

After paying one hundred seventy-five dollars for a one-way ticket to Atlanta, I was on my way.

CHANCE

Gia was on her tiptoes, straddling me as I sat on the couch. My dick was so far up inside of her that my ego was telling me that it was rubbing against her ribs.

No matter how many times I'd beat it up, that pussy was still so tight, cozy, and wrapped around my dick like a tight hug.

It was cool in the apartment, but my dick was warm and snug as it lay up inside her.

"Shit, baby." She cursed as she rode my dick. She twerked and bounced that ass just like she did on the stage every night. She held onto the back of the couch, giving herself leverage. I bit my bottom lip, trying desperately not to cum.

"Gawd damn." Gia was growling femininely through gritted teeth.

I started moving my hips up and down to encourage that cum to drip out of her.

"Oh my God!" She was panting heavily. "Oh shit!"

I looked at her face, but she didn't meet my eyes. Her head was back. Her eyes were closed tight. I could swear that I saw tears in the corner of her eyes.

Then suddenly, Gia hopped up and dropped to her knees. My dick was in her mouth before I could figure out what the fuck was going on. The sight of her licking her own pussy juice off my dick was like nothing I had ever seen before. I watched her with dilated eyes as my mouth gaped open. I fought hard not to cum.

She had been doing this shit since I got back; fucking the shit out of me. Along with cooking and spoiling a nigga by servicing me all day and night, she never stopped at the chance to fuck the shit outta me. She was using every method to show me how sorry she was.

I had told her over and over again, night after night, and every day that I forgave her. I would wake up and see the tears in her eyes as she stared at the ceiling. The guilt would wash over her suddenly as we were chilling. I told her all the time that it was cool and that we would figure things out. But shit, right at that moment, as she slurped and gagged on my dick, I wanted to scream at the top of my lungs that I forgave her.

"Shit!"

I threw Gia off as I hopped to my feet. I didn't know what else to do when I saw the figure of the woman walking by the window. I knew a dic when I seen one.

Gia didn't ask any questions. She followed me as I ran into the bedroom.

Then she closed the door. "What's wrong?!"

Naked, I paced the floor holding my head in my hands. "It's a fucking dic outside."

"How do you know?"

"She just walked by the fucking window!"

Just then, Gia's doorbell rang. As the chiming rang through

the house, I literally felt like I was going to shit bricks.

"Calm down, baby," Gia told me as she slipped on an oversized sleep shirt. "I'll take care of it. Just stay here."

Gia

Chance was right. I opened the door and the fair skinned woman introduced herself as Detective Howard.

"Hi, Detective. How may I help you?"

"Are you Gianna Michaels?"

"Yes. But you can call me Gia."

"May I come in?"

Before opening the door, I'd thrown anything resembling Chance into the nearest closest. I'd also sprayed Febreeze into the air to mask the smell of sex.

Still, as she entered my place, she eyed my hair. I was sure that it was disheveled from the good sex that this bitch had just interrupted.

"Am I interrupting something?"

I bashfully smiled and ran my fingers through my hair. "I was asleep."

"At three in the afternoon?"

"Yes, ma'am. I work nights at Sunset."

She nodded her head smugly as if she knew the place well. Then she snickered. "Raided that place a few times."

"I'm sure you have," I said with a laugh. "So, is this about Reginald?"

"Yes, it is. I am the detective assigned to the case."

I signaled for her to have a seat on the couch. I grimaced as she sat in the very same spot that Chance's naked ass was just sitting in. She was possibly marinating in the saliva that fell from my mouth as I sucked his dick.

"Would you like something to drink? A glass of water or something?"

"No, thank you. I won't be here long. I just have a few questions. I won't keep you long."

Nodding, I told her, "Okay."

"What happened with you and Reginald that made you come into the precinct? Did you know about this murder before?"

Immediately, I shook my head. "No way. He and I had only been messing around for a couple of months. Then suddenly he just up and said he had to leave town. No notice. No nothing. Just told me that he had a flight the next morning and was leaving."

"You have no idea where he was going or why?"

"No," I replied as I shook my head sadly. My sadness was real. The guilt I felt for kicking this shit off made me feel like shit. "So anyway, he came over to get some things before leaving. He sat one of his phones down. So I went through it. You know, I was trying to see was he leaving because of another woman or something. So I saw all these text messages between him and this Simone chick. I didn't read them all. But I did see a text referencing him 'popping' somebody for her. I was angry because I felt like I was with somebody that I didn't even know. So I let my anger get the best of me and I reported it."

"Have you ever heard him talk about Simone before?"

"No."

"Do you know anything about his past? Where he was from? Where he lived? Where his parents lived?"

I thought quickly to come up with something that was totally opposite of what I knew of Chance. "He's from Arizona. He'd just moved here when I met him. I don't know where he was staying exactly. Somewhere up North. We spent most of our time at my place. Then he eventually just moved on in."

"Have you heard from him again?"

"No. I'm not calling his ass. Fuck him."

"And he hasn't called you?"

"No."

Detective Howard sighed heavily and stood. "Well, if he does, would you let me know, please?"

"Sure will." Before she left, I wanted to get some information for Chance. I knew that he would want to know if there was any progress on the case. "So there was some truth to those messages that I found?"

"We did get transcripts of the text messages. They did mention the name Aeysha. Aeysha Walker was killed a few months ago in a drive by shooting."

"Did Reginald really do it?"

"I can't really say. We are investigating the case and we do have leads. So if you hear from him, please call me."

I assured her that I would while following her to the door. I couldn't get that bitch out of there fast enough.

"Thanks again," she said before leaving my doorway and walking down the steps.

"No problem. I'm glad to help."

I shut the door and bolted towards my bedroom. When I opened the door, I didn't see Chance anywhere.

"Chance! Chance!" I whispered his name in case the detective could hear me through the windows as she passed them by on her way to the car.

Suddenly, I heard noise under the bed. I giggled when I realized that it was Chance coming from underneath.

He began grilling me as he stood to his feet. "What she say?"

"She knows nothing about you. She's still asking about Reginald."

We sat close to one another on the bed as he asked, "Have they talked to Simone?"

"I don't know. But she did ask me if I ever heard you talk about her. And they know about Aeysha's murder."

"Shit. If they talk to Simone, it's a wrap."

"You think she'll tell on you? Telling on you is like telling on herself."

He shook his head hopelessly. "I don't know, bae. I don't put shit past that bitch."

I hugged him. He forced me down onto the bed. Then he laid

his head on my chest. I held him tightly.

I felt so bad for putting him in this predicament. I was ready to do any and every thing I could to help him get away with this. He didn't deserve to go to jail. Chance was an immature and lost boy when I met him. Now, he was a loyal man that had matured so much in the streets. I knew that if he could do it all again, he would never let that bitch talk him into murder. But, even in her old age, that bitch was still calculating and deadly. *She* was the one that deserved to pay for this.

Omari

"What's wrong, fam?"

I ended the call before Simone's voicemail could pick up. I slipped the phone in the pocket of my Billionaire Boys jeans and stood to leave.

I had been at the trap in Riverdale all day. I usually didn't sit at the spots for too long, but I didn't want to go back to the crib. I just couldn't stand looking at Simone's face. I couldn't even stand sleeping beside her.

But her attack still had me on pins and needles. I had called periodically to check on her throughout the day and she hadn't answered. The last time I heard from her was a text message earlier that day saying that she was going downtown to have lunch with some friends.

"I haven't heard from Simone. I been calling her all day. I'mma go home and check on her."

Capone stood as if he was leaving too. "I'll ride with you."

"It's all good, fam. I got it."

"Well, call me if you need me," he insisted as he sat back down.

"No doubt."

Paula shot me a goodbye from over the shoulder as she stood at the stove cooking a fresh batch of product. As I left out, I spotted Fred and some chick over in a dark corner on the porch.

I didn't even look their way as I told him, "I'm out."

Fred was breathing heavy as he barely said, "Ah ight, bro."

Lots of times the block boys got favors from the crack heads in exchange for a bag or two. I thought the shit was trife as hell, but that was on them. Even though they were outside, I would bet any amount of money that Fred was getting some head in that corner.

It's crazy how I was jealous of Fred. I wished to be as young and naive as he was so that I could do it all again. I thought Aeysha's death was the end. But it seemed as if it was only the beginning of foul and weird things happening to me. Simone's excuse for having that abortion was suspect. It just wasn't sitting right with me.

Her absence wasn't sitting right with me either. When I got home, the condo was pitch black. Her car wasn't in its usual spot. I looked through drawers to see if anything was missing, but they were still full of the expensive shit that she'd gotten with my drug money.

The thought of her being attacked again did enter my mind. She was an adult though, so I couldn't call the police and report her missing. I just hoped that she was pissed about our conversation that morning and was just giving me the silent treatment.

Chapter Five

Simone

After a twelve hour ride, four stops at nasty ass rest stops, three hours of this Hispanic baby crying who clearly had colic, and sitting by this fat bitch who kept sneezing, I finally arrived at the Greyhound station in downtown Atlanta.

The one thing that I could appreciate was the summertime temperatures compared to the stubborn spring air of Chicago. As I stepped outside of the Greyhound station, I felt the eighty degree weather in early May. The air was drenched with sunshine. I instantly took off the Givenchy hoodie that I was wearing to stay warm on the bus.

People were scattered everywhere; women and children, the homeless, and even men that looked like they had clearly just gotten out of jail.

I turned my nose up as a few guys with dirty white tee shirts, gold fronts, and lack of a clean lining looked me up and down and commented on my ass. But I quickly realized that turning my nose up was no longer an option. I had little to nothing, just like them.

Cabs lined the curb. It only took seconds for one to pull up.

"Take me to the nearest motel, please."

The cab driver took my duffel bag from me. As he placed it in the trunk, I climbed into the backseat of the Yellow Cab. With a deep breath, that was full of Muslim funk, I realized how bitchy karma truly was. She was a big, nasty, rude ass bitch that had found me and bit me clean in the ass.

Suddenly, I had traded places with Chance. Now I was the one broke and on the run, and he was comfortably in his hometown. Ironically, he was the only person that I could call, if anybody. As I thought about the amount of money in my pocket, I actually thought of calling him. I wanted to call his little ass and tell him that if he didn't leave town and send me some money that I would tell the cops everything. But for all I knew, he was the one that went to the cops in the first place.

As the cab whizzed down Windsor Street, I realized how real things had gotten so quickly. Just the other day, I was trying to figure out how to miraculously get pregnant. That was a task that now seemed so simple compared to the obstacle that I faced now.

My cell phone rang, scaring the shit out of me. I ignored Omari's call, turned the ringer off, and threw the cell into my Louis Vuitton tote. I told myself to change my number as soon as I got comfortable in the motel. I got goose bumps as I realized how, after destroying so many lives to get Omari, I was so quick to leave him when my own life was in jeopardy. Just a few days ago, I was so fixated on winning him that I couldn't imagine living without him. Now, I couldn't imagine going back home to him.

I wondered if he got the email that I sent while on the bus. I decided that it was best to break up with him, to blame my disappearance on my anger with him, and leave it at that.

I knew he'd buy it.

As I stared out of the window at my surroundings, I figured that things might not be as bad as they seemed. I didn't know what exactly the cops knew. I didn't know if they would ever be able to connect the dots. As long as they didn't know who Reginald Barner was, they had no concrete proof of anything. But what I did know was that I wasn't in Chicago to incriminate myself.

I was in a new city. And as long as I was careful, I would continue to outrun, outsmart, and dodge karma's bitch ass.

OMARI

I think I called Simone two hundred times. It was obvious that she was okay though. Her cell was still ringing, instead of going straight to voicemail, so she was safe enough to keep it charged.

I figured she called herself mad at me. She was probably at a hotel somewhere with an attitude. I didn't give a fuck. So much had happened that I was emotionally drained. I assumed that after Aeysha and Dahlia were gone, no other death would faze me. But it honestly fucked me up that Simone would kill our baby without telling me. For the first time in our relationship, I was questioning her loyalty and honesty, even her sanity.

I wondered what kind of bitch, who talked about nothing but pregnancy since I met her, would just get an abortion out of the blue. She wanted that baby, and me, way too much to just up and pull a move like that.

Something was definitely fishy about the shit. And she knew it. That's why she called herself acting like she was mad at me.

"I'm not finna chase her ass," I told myself as I climbed out of bed.

I knew she would come home eventually, so I decided to check in on my mama before I did my rounds at the spots that day.

Within the hour, I was ringing the doorbell at my mom's crib. Things had gotten a little bit better between us since Dahlia passed. Gradually, she understood my inability to go through another funeral. She and I had yet to visit her grave. Since the weather had finally officially changed, I figured she and I would one day soon take the time to go see Aeysha and Dahlia together.

My mother looked good when she finally opened the door holding a coffee cup and the remote. Age was looking so beautiful on her.

An eerie feeling suddenly came over me. With so much death surrounding me, I wondered if I would have the chance to age so gracefully.

"Hey, baby." She smiled at me as I entered the house. It was so great to see the genuineness in her face. She was one of few people that I could trust.

I bent down and allowed her to kiss me on the cheek. "Hey, mama."

"Good to see you. What are you doing here?"

"Brought you something."

I had gone through a lot and suffered a lot of loss to be able to do so, but it still felt honorable to be able to take care of my mama. Every time I paid a bill, I wished that Aeysha was there to see the man that I grew into. Every time I took Simone shopping, I wished that it was Aeysha instead.

After handing my mother an envelope that she slipped in the Bible on the coffee table, we sat down in front of her stories that played on the flat screen.

"I talked to Debbie."

Debbie is Ching's mother.

I chuckled. "I figured you would."

"Glad you all were able to take care of that."

I sighed in relief. "Me too."

"You were trippin'."

I laughed at my mother's slang. "Trippin'?"

"Yes."

She knew all about me robbing Ching and shooting at him. Ching called himself telling his mother so that Auntie Debbie could have my mother talk some sense into me. That's another thing that finally convinced me of his innocence.

He hadn't handled this in the streets like a hood nigga.

He told my mama!

That was because he was at his wit's end. He didn't want to hurt me, but he needed somebody to control my erratic ass.

"I was going through a lot. I still am."

My mother shook her head in disbelief. "I still can't understand why she was killed. Have you heard anything from the police?"

"A detective keeps calling me. I keep missing her call though."

"Missing her call? Omari, this is important and something you should stay on top of."

"Mama, I know, but all they have been doing is asking me the same generic questions over and over again. They don't have any evidence or any leads. What's the point in sending myself through that emotional shit over and over again just so they can feel like they are working the case?"

She couldn't argue with me, so she didn't.

"You wanna go see Aeysha and Dahlia this weekend?"

My mother couldn't hide the happiness in her heart. Tears of joy formed in her eyes that she tried to hold back on account of me. She tried to hide all emotions when it came to Dahlia and Aeysha because she knew that, since I was barely holding myself together, she had to hold herself together in front of me.

"I'd love to."

Simone

Night had begun to fall over the city of Atlanta.

My appetite left the day Detective Howard questioned me. But it finally decided to come back now that the coast seemed clear.

Before figuring out the cheapest thing to eat, I had to take care of a few things. I decided against changing my number. Instead, I turned my cell service off completely. I didn't want to risk being traced by a signal.

Then, I used the motel WiFi and workstation to log on to Facebook and delete every page that I'd logged onto from home. I had used the fake profiles to stalk many of my lovers and their women, including Aeysha. I hoped that deleting those pages would permanently delete any of that evidence.

After that, I left out of the motel in search of a McDonalds. I had been eating three course meals at five-star restaurants. I couldn't remember the last time I'd eaten at McDonalds. But now the dollar menu was looking very appetizing.

I walked down the main street. In five inch stiletto heels, distressed shorts, and a cami, I was sure that I looked like a hooker or a video hoe. Cars honked and men catcalled. After years of being insecure with my body, and myself, I had become so secure with my looks, new man, and new life. Now my stomach bulged from trying to look pregnant and that new man and new life was gone. I was vulnerable and knew that in a matter of days I wouldn't be able to afford to have a place to sleep.

Walking by a Bar Louie, I backtracked and figured that I would go inside. I would at least be able to afford a shot and an appetizer. I was craving alcohol more than food like never before.

Once inside, I nearly raced towards the bar.

"A shot of Jack. Neat, please."

Luckily for me, I heard some random guy say, "Give her two. I'm buying."

I turned my head to see who the gracious guy was while saying, "Thank you."

Two men sat a few bar stools down the way to my right. One was a gorgeous brown skinned over six feet tall glass of water. The other looked like his flunky. Sure, he was decent looking. But he was the 5'7" chunkier version of the other guy. Clearly, they were related. There was a lot of similarity in their facial features. Yet, there was nothing comparable when it came to their bodies. They looked like the Black version of Arnold Schwarzenegger and Danny Davito in the movie *Twins*.

Just my luck, Danny Davito was the one that smiled arrogantly and began to walk towards me, saying, "You're welcome, sexy. What's your name?"

Arnold Schwarzenegger stayed seated, discreetly looking me up and down, as Danny attempted to throw the lamest game that I have ever heard. I was more than willing to entertain him, however, if he continued to purchase drinks. I was in the mood to get as wasted as possible to temporarily escape my reality.

Danny's actual name was Teddy. He said it was a nickname and I clearly assumed why. Arnold was his brother, whose name was Jay.

Teddy was kind of cute, if chunky guys with potbellies and gold fronts are your thing. It was obvious that he'd lived his whole life trying to outshine his brother. He was well aware that he had to do a lot more to gain a woman's attention than Jay. Therefore, to keep my eyes on him, he made casual conversation about his major success flipping houses in the state of Georgia. He grossed over half a million dollars a year. He didn't have to tell me that. I could tell by the quality of diamonds in his ear, around his neck, and displayed on his wrist that he had money. However, because he talked about his business with such passion and intellect, I knew that he was smart money.

When he finally came up for air, from attempting to woo a woman that was seemingly out of his league with hints of what he was worth, he asked me about me. "You don't look like you're from around here. Where are you from?"

At this point, I was about six shots in, but I was on top of it. "I'm from Indiana, but I have been living in DC with my boyfriend."

"What are you doing all the way down in Atlanta?"

I allowed my eyes to drift and be overcome with sadness. "I had to leave," was all that I said because I knew that he would press the issue.

"Why?"

"My guy was beating me."

He sighed dramatically and shook his head in disgust.

"Yea, I know," I said with a sigh. "I kept trying to leave him. But with no friends or family there, I had nowhere to go. Even when I would go to a shelter, he would just find me and snatch me out of there. A few weeks ago, he busted my lip and tried to throw me down a flight of stairs. After that, I was done. I snuck out of the house in the middle of the night and caught a bus here."

"You got family here?"

"No. I don't have any family. I grew up as a ward of the state. Atlanta just seemed like a far enough place to go where he couldn't find me."

To add extra emphasis, I ran my fingers through my hair and dabbed at the corner's of my eyes with a napkin as if I was sopping up tears.

"Where are you staying?"

"In the motel a few doors down."

His demeanor switched to sympathy. "A girl looking like you shouldn't be staying in that motel, beautiful."

"My ex took care of the finances. He wouldn't let me work, so I didn't have much money of my own. All I have is a few dollars and the clothes that I left with. That motel is all that I can afford."

SIMONE

If karma was chasing me, luck was definitely still by my side. Fucking for money had never been an option, but desperate times called for desperate measures.

"Argh! Gawd damn. Shit, you got some good head, girl."

I moaned so that the vibrations in my throat would swim through his dick and ignite his arousal.

"Shit!"

I lifted my head, spit on his dick, and allowed the saliva to drool from my mouth to his dick. I did all of that while looking Teddy in the eyes.

His mouth gaped open. His eyes said words that couldn't come out because he was speechless.

The moment I saw Teddy's Bentley, I knew that, at the very least, he would be great at lending me a hand when I was in need while in Atlanta. He didn't mind giving away money. He'd kept me wasted the three hours that we sat and talked in Bar Louie. He purchased my meal. He even got an extra meal for me wrapped to go in case I got hungry during the night.

The way Jay looked at him scornfully on the low told me that Teddy had to be a goofy. He had money, but that money fed a self-esteem that was really low.

He walked me out and insisted on driving me to the motel since it had gotten so dark.

When we pulled up, I played so drunk and out of it. He played on my imaginary intoxication, kissing me and fondling my breasts with this slick grin on his chunky face like he was getting over, as if I was too drunk to know better.

He pulled his dick out. To my surprise, it was nice. It was always the short, average looking men with life size dicks that would have a bitch looking for him in the daytime with a flashlight.

But I only put my lips to it to ensure more free drinks and more free meals while I was in Atlanta.

"Shit! I'm cummin'!"

There was so much surprise in his sexual songs. He was shocked and excited at the same damn time.

He gripped the driver side door handle with his left hand as he released. "Arrrrrrrgh!!!"

I swallowed to ensure, if luck was still on my side while in Atlanta, a lot more than a free meal.

It was dangerous. It was nasty. It was a gamble.

But starving to death, wasting away in that motel, would have been way worse.

Chapter Six

OMARI

The last thing I remembered before going to sleep was calling Simone's phone one more time. I was caught off guard when the operator said that the number was no longer in service. I was in shock, thinking that Simone had gone too far with this mad shit.

That was the last thing I remembered before waking up to the sound of the doorbell ringing and the phone still in my hand. I was lying across the bed still fully clothed.

I looked around for signs of Simone and didn't see any evidence that she had been home. The condo was empty. Usually at this time of morning, I would hear the shower going, as she got ready for work. As I walked towards the door, I peeped that the bathroom was dark.

She hadn't been home.

That was shocking.

I couldn't believe that she was acting like this.

"Who is it?"

"Is Simone Campbell home?"

"Who's asking?"

I looked through the peephole and saw a badge being flashed.

I immediately knew something was wrong, so I opened the door in a hurry. Every time I'd seen the police recently, it was bad news.

"Simone isn't here."

The female detective looked surprised to see me. She also looked like she knew me. "Omari Sutton?"

"Yes."

"Oh. I didn't know you lived here. May I come in?"

"For what? What's going on?"

"Well, I was looking for Simone. I had questioned her the other day about Aeysha's murder. I had some more questions."

Instantly, I got curious. I couldn't hide how disturbed I was. "Simone didn't tell me that she had been questioned by anybody. And who are you? You aren't the detective who has been assigned to the case."

She actually gave me a chastising smirk before saying, "Well, if you would return my calls, you would know that we have new evidence and that I have been assigned to the case. I am Detective Howard."

Instantly, I felt embarrassed. "I'm so sorry," I told her as I let her in. "I've been meaning to call you back."

"I'm sure you assumed there was little urgency, considering how slow the case has been going. But, like I said, we have new evidence."

"What is the new evidence?"

We sat at the kitchen table. Instead of answering my

question, she slowly looked around the condo as if she was taking it all in.

Then she asked, "How long have you been living here with Simone?"

"Just a couple of months."

"You moved on pretty quickly after Aeysha's death." She saw the instant change in my demeanor in response to her statement. She added, "No offense."

I didn't even have a response. She was right. I was too ashamed to admit that it was so easy for me to physically move on after Aeysha's death because I was already sleeping with Simone.

But it was like Detective Howard read my mind. "Were you and Simone sleeping together while you were with Aeysha?"

My chest lost all mass, and I nodded shamefully.

That gave her the answer that she was looking for, so she continued pressing me. "What kind of relationship did you and Simone have? Did she think that she was your girlfriend?"

"*Aeysha* was my woman," I told her. "I was with her for seven years. That was heart. I know that it may not seem like it, since I was cheating on her. But honestly that was just the type of man that I was. I dipped off on Aeysha, but I loved her and would never leave her. These chicks knew that."

"Did Simone know that?"

I nodded.

"So Simone knew about Aeysha?"

"She knew that I had a woman that I wasn't about to leave."

"But she didn't know her?"

"No."

"That you know of."

"Simone didn't know Aeysha, period. I didn't play around like that. I didn't mix the two like that. They didn't know the same people. Simone didn't even know where I lived. She didn't even know Aeysha's name for a long time."

Simply, the detective nodded as if she was taking it all in.

"I'm sorry, but what does this have to do with the questions you have about Aeysha's murder?"

It was funny the way the detective looked at me. I couldn't really peg what the look in her eyes meant. She looked like she was trying to find the right words to say.

"Have you seen Simone?"

"No, actually. I think she got mad at me and left. I haven't seen her in two days. Her stubborn ass won't answer the phone."

Detective Howard's eyebrows moved with suspicion. "Why would she get mad and leave?"

"She did some shit to piss me off. I been treating her kinda funny for the past few days. We got into it the last time that I saw her. When I came home, she was gone."

"When was this?"

"Day before yesterday."

"Has she ever mentioned the name Reginald Barner to you?"

"No. Not at all."

This line of questioning had my heart racing with anxiety. "What does all of this have to with Aeysha's death? Who is Reginald Barner?"

"I can't discuss that with you. Not at this time."

My chest heaved as I made my own assumptions. "Did he kill Aeysha?!"

Detective Howard placed her hand on the table to calm me down. "I am just following up on some things, Omari. I promise you, when I have some concrete evidence, when I have someone in custody, you will know."

My mind was racing. My head was spinning. I didn't understand why Simone was of interest. It made me sick trying to figure it all out.

Whoever the fuck Reginald Barner was, he had to die.

Just for the reference to Aeysha's death, he had to die.

Point blank.

Eboni

Since Detective Howard left my house last week, Omari had heavily been on my mind.

The fact that Simone came up in the investigation of Aeysha's death was fucking with me. The fact that Omari was now dating Simone was fucking with me even more.

I didn't know much of Omari's side of things with him and Aeysha. We barely talked when we hooked up. But from what Aeysha told me, he was a loving boyfriend that had the can't-help-its when it came to side pussy.

I never doubted that he loved Aeysha, even when he was fucking me. It was apparent that she came first. But what possibly didn't come first, second, or ever was a family to a man that wanted to be in the streets, especially a man with new money.

I wasn't going to wait for the police to figure it out. I had it all figured out already. Plus, it was time that I hollered at Omari anyway.

And since Terrance shockingly still had the kids, I strapped my baby in his car seat and headed to Riverdale.

Omari still wasn't answering my calls, which was even more suspicious. I hadn't done shit to him by visiting, but maybe my visit did something to him.

Just my luck, when I pulled up, Omari's Challenger was parked out front, along with a few other rides. Nervously, I parked, got my baby out of the back seat, and walked towards the front porch where some young nigga was posted.

"Is Omari here?"

Despite me holding a newborn swaddled in a blanket, he still looked me up and down longingly. There was nothing to long for. My stomach still looked at least five months pregnant. I was still twenty pounds overweight. Moving around with the other kids had helped with beginning to get some of the weight off. I had been attempting to do Zumba during the kids' naps, which had been a major fail so far.

"What's up, mama? I'm Fred. What's your name?"

Fred was clearly a kid. He couldn't have been more than eighteen.

"I'm Eboni. Is it okay that I go in? Is Omari's girl here?"

He looked at me curiously and then laughed. "Nah. You cool. They don't live here. This is the spot, girl. You good."

With confusion, I followed Fred into the house. Another young guy was sitting at the table. An older white woman was at the table across from him, bagging up what looked like cocaine. That's when this being "the spot" made sense to me.

"What's up, boss. She here to see Omari."

I recognized the second guy from my first visit.

"Oh, hey. Aeysha's home girl. Omari is in the front. C'mon."

As I followed him down the hall, I remembered that his name was Capone. Looking at the house's features, it saddened me that this was the house that Aeysha was once so happily looking forward to moving into.

Omari was on the couch, clutching a red cup, and staring aimlessly into the flat screen that was reflecting highlights from last season's basketball games.

It was crazy how, though time had passed, the stress in his eyes had gotten way worse. He used to stress over paying the bills when he and Aeysha stayed above me. Then, no sooner than he had something to rejoice about, deathly circumstances brought back the pain and sadness in those beautiful gray eyes.

When he looked up and saw me, I actually saw some relief in eyes that appeared so tired.

"What's up, Eboni? What you doin' here?"

He was speaking to me, but looking curiously at the bundle that I was holding. He also looked at me, at the change in my once toned and in-shape appearance.

Before I could answer, he asked, "You had a baby?"

"Yea," I said with a heavy breath. "I had a baby, Omari."

He laughed. "Damn, girl. You done had *another* baby?!"

Even Capone laughed as he walked out of the living room and went back down the hall towards the kitchen.

Just as Omari stood to greet me, I let it out. "*We* had another baby."

He stumbled back a bit. He even squinted, as if squinting would help him understand what the fuck I just said.

To clarify, I removed the blanket from Jamari's face, revealing his uncanny likeness to Omari; the luscious dark hair, slim bone structure, full lashes, and gray eyes.

Swear to God, I wasn't expecting Omari's tears. I wasn't expecting him to break down as he came closer and took Jamari from me with eagerness. He sat down full of shock. I sat next to him on the couch as he cradled him to his chest.

"What... When..." Omari was at a loss for words, and that was to be expected. I was expecting him to be extremely caught off guard. I had a lot of explaining to do.

"Omari, when I got pregnant, I honestly wasn't going to keep him. Aeysha was pregnant. You guys were so happy. I should have been more respectful of those things before, but finding out that I was pregnant put a lot of things into perspective." He was listening to me, but he wasn't looking at me. He was gazing into Jamari's eyes, who had awakened at his father's touch and was staring back at him. "But before I could get an abortion, Aeysha was killed. Something just couldn't bring me to kill my baby. I realized how precious life was. When I came here that day a few months ago, I wanted to tell you that I was pregnant, especially after hearing about Dahlia. I wanted to give you some life back. But I just didn't know how to explain myself. And I've been trying to call you ever since, but I can't get through to you."

For the first time, he looked at me. "You haven't been calling me."

"Yes, I have. Ever since the last time I was here. I wanted to tell you about the baby."

OMARI

The baby. He was beautiful. He looked just like me. His eyes put me in the mind of Dahlia, which made me weak.

"I've been trying to call you for months. Your phone keeps hanging up on me. I figured you blocked me."

"Block you? How do I do that?"

Eboni shook her head at my ignorance.

I was too wrapped up in the baby to even pay attention to what she was talking about. "What's his name?"

"Jamari."

I could have died. "Jamari?! What kinda ghetto ass shit is that?!"

We both laughed.

"Don't talk about my baby's name!"

"We gon' have to change that shit. He needs to have my last name anyway."

Eboni sighed, as if she had so much to say in response. I knew that she had a lot on her mind. There was a lot behind and ahead of her having my baby. But I didn't care about any of that. I just wanted to enjoy him. I just wanted to inhale the smell of Baby Magic. I only wanted to feel the silkiness of his curly hair against my fingertips.

"Omari, a detective came to see me the other day. She was a new detective and she had new evidence."

I cleared my throat, attempting to clear the ball out of it that appeared every time I thought about Detective Howard's visit. "She came to see me today."

Eboni seemed relieved. "She did?! Did she ask you about Simone?"

"She talked to you about Simone? What did she ask you?"

I couldn't believe that Detective Howard had so much interest in Simone. I didn't understand why our relationship was that important to Ayesha's case. It was making my guilt for fucking with Simone before and right after Aeysha's death that much worse.

"She showed me some pictures and asked me if I recognized anyone. One of the pictures was Simone. I told her about Simone being at Bar Louie with me and Aeysha..."

My shock interrupted her. "What?"

"That's what I have been trying to tell you too! A little while before Aeysha got killed, we went to Bar Louie. Simone sat right at the bar and talked to us. She said she was a hiring manager and took Aeysha's number. She didn't say that her name was Simone though."

When Eboni tried to tell me this a few months ago, it sounded too trippy to believe. But looking into her eyes as she told me, I didn't have any choice but to believe her. There was so much passion in her eyes when she talked about it.

But, hell, Simone had the same passion in her eyes when she talked about a baby that wasn't even there anymore.

"Are you sure?"

"I swear. Does she drive a silver Camaro?"

"She use to. She was in it that day?"

"I don't know about all that. But Detective Howard asked me if I recognized a silver Camaro. I saw that car on the block just sitting a lot before Aeysha got killed."

It was possible that Simone followed me home a few times. She was so high strung when it came to me that I could totally see her tailing me to see where I lived.

"Did the detective ask you about some Reginald dude?"

"Yea," she answered. "But I have never heard of him."

My head was spinning. I handed Jamari to Eboni. I stood and began to pace the floor.

"You think Simone had something to do with it?"

"Hell nah. How could she?"

Eboni eyed me curiously but replied, "Hell, I don't know. But why is she coming up in the investigation?"

"If they are digging and looking for evidence, Simone would come up, especially if they are looking into my background. I was fucking with her while I was with Aeysha – heavy."

Eboni sighed dramatically and shook her head. "Who weren't you fucking, Omari?"

Luckily, Capone appeared in the doorway before I had the chance to respond to Eboni's disapproving eyes.

"You ready to roll?"

Capone and I were on our way to the spot out south. We had just gotten a new shipment of heroin in and needed to take Paula over to cook it up for us. We also needed to collect money from the block boys.

"Give me two minutes, bro," I told Capone.

With that, Capone left out of the doorway, not even noticing Jamari. I figured I'd tell him about my son during the ride out south.

I gave Eboni a stern look. "*Call me.*"

I wanted to see my baby as much as I could. I also wanted to check up on Eboni. I knew that she was struggling with three kids, so she was definitely struggling now with four.

"I have been!" Then Eboni took out her phone. She began punching numbers and then put the phone on speaker.

The line rang once. Then it seemed as if the call was answered right before it abruptly ended.

"See?! It hangs up on me!" Then she put her hand out. "Give me your phone, Omari."

I handed it to her with no reluctance. I didn't know shit about phones. I just wanted to send text messages, make calls, and look at naked bitches on Vine.

However, Eboni was going through the phone like a champ. She knew where everything was.

"You blocked me, motherfucka!"

I looked at her like she was crazy. "No, I didn't!"

She turned the screen of the phone towards me. It reflected some Mr. Number shit and a list of numbers. One of the numbers was Eboni's. I snatched the phone when I realized that the other numbers belonged to my sister, Erica, and her husband, Tre.

"What the fuck?!"

Eboni wasn't buying it. She looked at me like I was fronting.

"This is my sister's number. Why the fuck would I block my sister?" I handed the phone back to her. "Can you fix it? Unblock all those numbers."

Eboni was tapping on the screen as she asked, "You mean to tell me that you didn't know shit about this?"

"I don't know nothin' about no apps and shit. Simone probably did that shit, man." She had to. I remembered her irritation with Eboni texting me, thinking that I would start cheating on her like I did Aeysha. I also remembered her irritation with my sister and Tre.

That damn Simone was really turning out to be a motherfuckin' trip.

Chapter Seven

Simone

I had been in Atlanta for a week. To make the time held up in the motel go by, I took a lot of the Vicodin and muscle relaxers prescribed to me after Jimmy whooped my ass.

It was crazy how prior to leaving Chicago, I thought that I would die without Omari. I thought that my life would be meaningless if I wasn't waking up to him every day. But now that I had no choice but to move on, there was no pain in losing him. There was only determination to keep my freedom.

I did miss him though. His smell had been replaced by the stench of cheap cleaning products that overwhelmingly took over the hotel room. The space next to me was no longer the chocolate amazing creation that I was use to waking up to every morning. There were no massive arms holding me. There were no lips kissing me in the morning.

The memories of Omari ran away as the telephone rang.

I knew that it could only be one person.

"Hello?"

"Damn, baby. So you just make a brotha feel good and disappear? Just like a nigga!"

I held in a chuckle as I got comfortable under the dated flower bedding of the motel bed. It was three in the afternoon, but I could do nothing but sleep.

Financially, I really had no other option.

"I'm sorry, Teddy. I've been feeling some kinda way for the last couple of days."

I was lying. I mean, yes, I was feeling some kind of way. Running from a murder charge would do that to you. But I had been ignoring the motel room phone when it rang on purpose. Every time it rang, I knew it was Teddy. He was the only person with the number. He'd even come by and knocked on the door twice.

I was ignoring him on purpose. I needed him and his money eating out of the palm of my hand. So I had to further lower his self esteem by ignoring him. I needed the distance to fill his mind with further insecurities that he would be insistent on making go away by showing me otherwise.

"Feeling some kind of way? Why?"

"I miss my family," I said with sadness engulfed in the sound of my voice. "I'm so lonely here. I think I want to go back home."

"Back home? Not to that nigga, I know."

Purposely, I allowed silence to speak for me.

"C'mon now. You can't go back to that kind of treatment."

"I don't have many options. My money is running out. I can't be on the street."

"Baby girl, look, I know you don't know me from a can of

paint, so you probably ain't even tryin' to hear what I got to say. But you can do so much better than a nigga putting his hands on you. You gotta stay strong. Have you been out?"

I whined, "No. I haven't been up to it."

"C'mon now. You gotta get outside and enjoy the 'A, baby!"

I giggled. His southern drawl made anything that he said sound so charming. Teddy lacked in the looks department. He was no Omari and his physique needed a lot of work. But what he lacked in the physical, he made up for with hella personality and coins.

"Put some clothes on. I'm coming to get you."

I was sure that Teddy only wanted some more head and even some pussy. But because he was obviously a goofy, he was willing to do and spend way more to get it than the average man.

Yet, in order to seal the deal, I continued to play hard to get. "I don't know. I mean, I don't have much money. I'm just not in the mood."

"As long as you're with me, money is not an issue, baby."

Chance

Playfully, I wrapped my arms around Gia's waist as we walked out of the Walgreens. She was holding the milk and orange juice that she needed for the house. I nibbled on her neck as we walked, together, through the automatic doors.

She giggled. "Stop, boy!"

She looked so good though. I just couldn't keep my hands off of her. It was a sunny day. It was about seventy degrees. The weather was perfect.

If only life was as perfect. But being with Gia honestly made me feel like life was. Looking at her in those leggings and crop top was like watching one of God's baddest creations. Her waist was the tiniest thing I'd ever seen. Her booty deserved its own soundtrack. She hadn't combed her hair that day. It was all over her head in fallen curls that she'd slept on. She didn't feel like putting on shoes, so she had on them damn flips flops from the beauty supply store. But she still looked like perfection.

"You wanna hang out today?"

I stayed on the block hustling as much as I could. And with Gia dancing at night, we rarely spent time socializing. We were usually sleep or fucking.

"Sure," she told me as we got in her car. "What you wanna do?"

"It's a nice out. Let's go downtown."

She smiled at the sound of that. "Let's go to the Cheesecake Factory. I'm hungry."

As I started the car, I teased her. "Cheesecake Factory?! You ain't gettin' no Cheesecake Factory. Tuh! You got regular pussy, girl. You want some Harold's Chicken?"

She erupted in laughter before smacking my face playfully as I pulled out of the parking lot and into traffic.

"Whateva, nigga!"

"Nah, for real tho. Cheesecake Factory is cool."

I honestly would have done whatever I could for that girl. I would have taken her anywhere. It was crazy how going through all this drama with the murder and the cops was bringing us closer. Despite what I was facing, I didn't leave her. She saw that and rocked with me even heavier because of it. Despite her knowing what I'd done, she hadn't left me. That was amazing to me. I had family that had left me for much less.

I rocked with her even heavier because of it.

"*Fuck.*" I cursed as my eyes fell onto the rear view mirror. "The police are behind me."

Just like a woman, Gia immediately turned around and looked.

"Those aren't streets cops either. Those are detectives," she said sadly.

I glanced at her and saw panic filling in her eyes.

"Be cool."

But she didn't stay cool. She winced. "Gun it."

I laughed. "Are you crazy?"

"They are on bullshit, Chance. You didn't run a light. You aren't speeding…"

"Gia, be cool," I insisted as I turned off the radio.

Since Detective Howard left a little over a week ago, we hadn't heard shit. Gia and I were going on with life as it had been before that day I tried to leave Chicago. I was serving at the trap day and night, trying to hustle up enough bread to split. Gia was at Sunset, every night, trying to do the same. She was ready to leave too. Living in this suspense was more than nerve wrecking. Every time the doorbell rang, every time we saw a cop, we saw my life ending.

A few days ago, I heard Omari telling Capone that he couldn't find Simone. He hadn't heard from her or seen her. She hadn't even been to her own house. Gia and I figured that Detective Howard had also questioned her. We wondered if she had been arrested or had run.

I knew I was next.

I guess today was the day.

"Maybe it's some drug shit," I tried to convince myself.

Gia slid her hand on my leg as she stared out of the rear view mirror. "Maybe they aren't about to stop you."

"They've been following me for three blocks."

Deadly silence filled Gia's 300. All we could hear was the air conditioner blowing and faint thuds under the car as we hit pot holes.

As the sirens began, our breathing stopped and Gia's tears started.

"Keep going, Chance," she urged.

I laughed nervously. "You want me to run, bae?"

She was crying by now. "Hell yea."

"Calm down," I insisted as I pulled over to the curb.

She dried her tears. Then Gia looked like she wanted to hop in my lap, take the wheel, and drive away herself. Looking through the side mirror, I watched the same detective approach the driver's side of the car with her gun drawn. It was Detective Howard, and she wasn't alone. There was a detective with her. He was a tall white guy, who appeared on Gia's side of the vehicle with his gun drawn as well.

I rolled the window down and then placed my hands on the steering wheel.

Detective Howard bent down, looked at Gia, and smiled. "This Reginald, Gia?"

Gia smacked her lips, folded her arms across her chest and simply stared out of the windshield.

"My name is Chance Rogers, ma'am," I told her as I handed her my driver's license. "Why are you stopping me? Did I run a stop sign?"

Detective Howard reached into her pocket and pulled out

what looked like a photo. She looked at it and then looked at me.

"Reginald, step out of the vehicle."

"My name is…"

"Step out of the vehicle! NOW!"

Gia jumped at the sudden sound of Detective Howard being aggressive. I could hear her crying. I got out of the car before Gia could say or do anything that gave us away or made us look suspicious.

"We're taking you to the precinct for some questions," was what Detective Howard said as she grabbed my arm. "Put your hands behind your back."

I did as I was told. Purposely, I didn't say anything. I looked into the back window, watching Gia twisted in the front seat. She sadly watched as the other detective met us where we stood and assisted Detective Howard in cuffing me.

Omari

"Omari, you okay?"

My mother looked at me curiously as I stared blankly at the screen of my phone.

"I'm okay. Just give me a second."

I hadn't checked my email in over a week. I rarely went online unless I was paying a bill or buying something. That day, I was checking the tracking for some speakers I'd ordered when I saw an email from Simone. She'd sent it over a week ago; the day she never came back home.

Omari,

I'm going out of town for a while. I need a break. I'm tired of this shit. I can't take it anymore. It's been a year and I am still coming second to your woman. I've been there for you. I've had your back. I've put you first when you never put me first. But what hurt the most was the fact that you couldn't even put my baby first. You couldn't even acknowledge your life with me enough to come to the doctor, to act happy about the baby. I killed my baby because of Aeysha and Dahlia's constant influence on you. I am tired of their memory running my life. I'm still your side bitch, and I'm tired of it. I'm leaving. I need a break.

I'm selling the condo, so I suggest you move out.

"You gotta be kidding me," I mumbled as I dropped the phone in the cup holder.

My mother looked at me and asked. "What's wrong?"

"Nothing. It's not important. Let's do this."

I got out of the car and made it to the passenger side. I opened the door and helped my mother out. It was a beautiful day in the city of Chicago– way too beautiful to be in a cemetery. Simone always claimed that I put Aeysha and Dahlia first.

However, there I was, standing in front of their graves and all I could think of was Simone. I couldn't wrap my head around her ways lately. Things were getting weirder and weirder.

I didn't even know if she'd been back to her house. Since she wasn't answering my calls, I stopped trying to call days ago and had been staying at the trap.

If she wanted to leave, that was fine. I had no energy to argue with her about how I was grieving the loss of the love of my life and my child.

If she was too self-absorbed to understand that, fuck her.

My mother suddenly caught my eye. Initially, I thought that she was falling. But she was kneeling down next to Dahlia. Dahlia was buried in the winter. Back in March, the snow finally melted and revealed the headstone that I purchased with a beautiful picture of her on it, along with a picture of Aeysha pregnant with her.

This was my mother's first time seeing it.

Weeping filled the silence. To comfort my mother, I simply stood behind her and put my hand on her shoulder.

I fought my own tears. I was tired of crying. I was tired of hurting and grieving. For once in the last year, I had something to be thankful for. I looked down at the picture of Dahlia on her grave and saw so much of Jamari in her face. I thanked God for giving me yet another chance at having a family. I swore a silent vow that I would take care of them how I should.

Chance

I sat in the interrogation room for three hours.

They took my phone. They secluded me in the small room without telling or asking me anything. It felt like I was already sitting in a cell.

"Mister Rogers."

Detective Howard entered the room with her partner, Detective Ingram, following her.

I snickered when she called me Mr. Rogers. Finally, this bitch actually believed what my name was.

She didn't say anything else as she sat across from me. Detective Ingram sat in a chair a few feet away in the corner of the room. It was apparent that Detective Howard was taking the lead in this case.

She reached into a file, took out a photo, and slid it in front of me.

"That is a photo of you and Simone Campbell in a gas station an hour after the death of Aeysha Walker on October 30, 2013."

She didn't have to tell me what the fuck the photo was. I knew what it was.

"This is a copy of the text message transcripts between Reginald Barner and Simone Campbell since the death of Aeysha Walker that reference Reginald murdering Aeysha for Simone. Reginald Barner was reportedly living with Gianna Michaels up until a week and a half ago. Yet, these are images of you going in and out of Sunset with Gia that we got from the club's surveillance cameras." As she continued, she slid distorted images of a man entering Sunset and leaving with Gia. Though distorted, it was obvious that it was me.

With a heavy sigh, Detective Howard looked dead into my eyes. "What is your relationship with Simone Campbell?"

A lot of things crossed my mind. I wondered if I should be honest. Finally, ninety-nine percent of the things in my life were going right. Gia had her issues, but I had a good and beautiful woman. I was getting money. I was amongst a crew that was beginning to be like the brothers that I never had. But this murder was keeping me from fully enjoying any of that. There was a constant elephant in the room when I was around Omari. I could never fully relax when I was with Gia because I never knew when the cops were coming.

I was ready for this to be over. I had been running, dodging, and ducking for a year.

I was tired.

"Am I under arrest?"

"That has yet to be determined," Detective Howard told me. "And it depends a lot on what you have to tell me."

We stared each other down for a few seconds. She was waiting on me to give her something. I was waiting on my mind to give me what to say.

"I want a lawyer," was all that came to mind that made any sense to me.

She tried to hide her disappointment. I wasn't about to go down like that though. This evidence that they had was weak as hell. They couldn't arrest me with this shit.

"So you're going to go down for this all by yourself?" Detective Howard was no longer cool. Her poise was gone. There was passion in her eyes that she had once been successful in masking. "Don't sit there looking all cool like you can beat this. You wouldn't be here unless we had enough evidence to convict you. We ran your name. You lived at Lexington House where Simone Campbell worked. You're connected all up in this murder, Chance. The dots are connecting. And they will continue to connect until they form a very straight arrow that points to you."

When I didn't flinch or budge, it pissed her off. She went into her binder and pulled out more photos. She began slapping them on the table. They were photos of the crime scene. Blood was all over the concrete. There were images of Aeysha's bloody coat and clothes that had been torn from her body before they transported her into the ambulance.

"She was seven months pregnant! She will never see her child that she carried for months! And for what?! For what, Chance?! For twenty-five thousand dollars?!"

She snickered when she saw my expression change at the mention of the money that Simone paid me to kill Aeysha.

"Yea, I know about the twenty-five thousand dollars that Simone took out of her savings two days before Aeysha's murder."

I reiterated, "I want a lawyer," as I sat back and folded my arms across my chest.

Detective Howard slammed the binder down on the table. "Fine. Stand up, Mr. Rogers. You're under arrest for the murder of Aeysha Walker."

Simone

Teddy picked me up a few hours ago. First, he took me to dinner at Gladys. I had my first taste of Chicken and Waffles, and it was amazing. Then we went to Lenox Mall. Being at places that I had heard about over and over again in rap songs was so much fun. I grew up in Chicago and stayed in Chicago. I hadn't ventured out or gone out of town. The furthest I'd gone was Indianapolis with Omari or small towns for business trips with Lexington House.

Being in Atlanta was like starting anew. It was a fresh start. Despite being broke, the change was refreshing. Now that I had taken myself out of the norm, things appeared to be so different. I was no longer waiting on some man that I was fucking to pay attention to me. I was no longer cringing in the shadows of Aeysha, Erica, and every other bitch that had the hearts of my men. Suddenly, I was able to shake off that insecurity and be a big girl.

We ended the night at Stokers, a gentlemen's club, a little outside of Atlanta in Clarkston, Georgia. The weed smoke was thick. The men were the hood's finest. Despite the fact that Stroker's worst stripper looked way better than Chicago's best stripper, it was obvious that this was Atlanta's hole in the wall strip club. Yet, every stripper's face was beat to the back row of the church. Obviously, there was a makeup artist in the back making sure that their faces looked just as good as their fake saline asses.

"Whad up, bro?"

I tore my attention away from the stripper twirling on the pole and glanced over at Teddy. He was standing and greeting Jay, who'd just entered the club with a badass chick on his arm. She looked like a stripper her damn self. Despite having a woman on his arm, he still fought to keep his eyes off of me... or maybe my cleavage. I was wearing an orange bandage dress that pushed my breasts up to my damn neck.

Despite Jay being a perfect sight, despite him being able to make my body flow like a river on sight, he was obviously a fucking creep. The way he looked at me, despite me being with his brother, told that he was a true asshole who was probably the source of Teddy's insecurity.

Chapter Eight

Omari

The next day, I went to Simone's condo early in the morning. I kinda hoped that I would bump into her while I was getting my things. Honestly, I had no urge to convince her to stay with me. She was right. I had always put Aeysha first. I had no guilt about that. I *should* have put Aeysha first. Aeysha was the love of my life. I had no guilt about how I grieved her and Dahlia.

I did, however, want to apologize for wasting a year of Simone's life. All in all, she had my back no matter what. She was the reason why I had the money that I had. She was the reason why I was able to live on, though barely, after Aeysha's death. She stood by my side, financed my come up, and even helped raise my baby. She'd done all of that when I wouldn't even commit to her until I had no other option.

However, she never showed up while I got every item of clothing, every electronic device, and the secret stash of cash that I hid in the floorboard under the bed. I didn't want to have to come back. Aeysha died, and I dealt with it by focusing on chasing a man that wasn't guilty. Dahlia died, and I didn't deal with it at all.

It was time for me to grieve, to take care of myself, without Simone. It was fucked up that it had come to this, but I was honestly glad that she had broken up with me. She'd done the dirty work that I was never man enough to do.

Once I stored the bags full of belongings into the trunk, I got into the driver's seat and pulled off while dialing Eboni's number. She'd kept her promise and called as much as she could. She'd sent me tons of pictures of Jamari that she managed to take since he'd been born. But I hadn't seen Jamari again yet.

"Hello?" When she answered, she sounded tired and drained, like she always did since she spent most of her day chasing after very hyper kids.

"What's up, Eboni? What you doin' today?"

"Nothing. What are you doing?"

I sighed heavily as I pulled off. Funny thing, it was a sigh of relief. "Just got my stuff out of Simone's crib."

"Huh?"

I laughed at her confusion. "Yea, she broke up with me."

"You still haven't seen her?"

"She actually broke up with me a week ago. She sent me an email. Told me to get out of her crib."

"An email? That chick is so strange."

Sarcastically, I chuckled. "Stranger things have happened."

Eboni fell silent in the irony.

"Why don't you come over today?"

"I have my kids."

"So."

"I can't have all my kids in your trap house, Omari."

"C'mon," I begged. "Please? I wanna see the baby."

"Come over here."

"I'm not ready."

The day Aeysha died, I hid at my mother's house until the day that I had to move out of me and Aeysha's apartment. That day was just as painful as the day she died. Having to box Aeysha's clothes, being overwhelmed with her scent, was horrible.

Just the thought of it brought tears to my eyes.

Eboni sighed and gave in. "Okay, Omari."

"I won't let the block boys in and I'll tell Paula to cook over at the other spot. Guess I need to find me a place so you can bring him over without worrying about it."

I was willing to do whatever I had to do to do it right this time. God had given me yet another chance at a family. Jamari would never replace Dahlia, but the idea of having a son was replacing sadness with feeling proud and humble. Eboni and I were far from being in a relationship, but she and her kids were like family. Being around Eboni and her children reminded me so much of being with Aeysha. I was starting to believe that maybe engulfing myself in Aeysha's memory, rather than masking the pain with anger, would help me grieve.

SIMONE

My hangover was lethal. I attempted to open my eyes, but the bright Georgia sun shining through the picture window blinded me.

The snoring caught me off guard. It sounded like there was a bear in the bed next to me. Slowly, I turned my head. Teddy's mouth was gaped open. His fronts flashed at me. His potbelly was nothing in comparison to the six-pack I usually woke up to.

I grimaced and slowly turned back around, attempting to keep my head from spinning.

I couldn't remember shit. Not a damn thing. The last thing I remembered was Teddy telling me that I didn't have to stay at the motel last night. I looked under the sheet that I was wrapped in. I was completely naked. My vagina felt mutilated. I figured that Teddy and I had had sex.

The urge to pee forced me out of the surprisingly very soft sheets. No matter how delirious I was, I knew Mulberry silk when I felt it.

I staggered out of bed as quietly as I could, wondering where the hell the bathroom was. Then I saw an opened door leading to what I assumed to be the master bath. As I entered, I was completely overwhelmed. I instantly woke up and came to my senses. The bathroom was just as big as the bedroom. The seven by four foot whirlpool Jacuzzi tub was calling my name. Instead of a sink, there was a romantic his and her double vessel vanity sink. After peeing, I slid the shower door open and stepped inside of it with amazement. There were multiple showerheads, even one above my head. There were even massage jets and seating!

As I left the bathroom, I wondered what the hell the rest of the house looked like.

Teddy was no longer snoring. He was still lying down, but he was staring into the screen of his iPhone.

When he noticed me, he smiled and said, "Good morning."

"Good morning. Did I wake you?"

"Yea. I'm going back to bed though," he said, setting his phone on the nightstand. "It's too fucking early."

I giggled while telling him, "Its twelve o'clock."

"That's early as hell. We didn't get in until five."

Curiously, and quite shamefully, I asked, "Did we have sex?"

I wasn't playing my usual games. For the life of me, I really couldn't remember.

Teddy chuckled. "I figured you was drunk."

I grimaced. "Oh God."

"Yea, we had sex, girl! We were coming up the stairs and you attacked me! You started sucking my dick."

I palmed my forehead.

Teddy laughed at my embarrassment while explaining, "I told you let's take it upstairs. And you was like 'no, fuck me right here'. I knew you were wasted then."

I grinned at him mischievously. "So you took advantage of

me?"

"You made me! You tried to sit on my dick without me even having a rubber on."

"Oh my God! You did wear a rubber though, right?"

"Of course I did."

I sighed with relief and stared out of that beautiful picture window. The view of the woods was amazing scenery. Then my eyes fell on the dreamy deck that surrounded an in ground pool and adjoining hot tub.

"Where am I? Like what city am I in?"

Again, Teddy laughed at my confusion. "We are still in Atlanta, but you're in Druid Hills."

"Druid Hills?! Like the singing group?!"

Giggling, he answered, "Yes, baby. Like the singing group."

"How much did I drink?"

"I don't know, but you were pretty turnt up."

It was so sad that listening to his voice and staring out of that window was like heaven, but I couldn't turn to look at him without being horribly disappointed.

"You hungry?"

"I'm starving."

"Can you cook?"

"Can I? Of course I can." Then I got the hint. "Do you have some food for me to cook?"

"Sure do."

"Where are my clothes?"

He laughed saying, "Probably still on the stairs."

I had to laugh as well. "Wow."

He was right, though. As he turned over and got comfortable under the sheets, I made my way out of the bedroom. I walked by mounds of new shoeboxes and shopping bags. He had a beautiful home, but it was kept up in the way that only a single man would.

In the hallway, I walked by three additional bedrooms. I peeked inside each one, seeing that they were fully furnished but untouched. Sure enough, my clothes were sprawled randomly on the winding staircase. I imagined my drunken self seeing this house, losing my mind, and filling up with lustful greed. I gathered my dress, bra, panties, and heels and continued down the staircase, giggling at myself.

This house was remarkable. It was the most beautiful thing that I had ever seen. His man cave was architecturally designed to resemble a log cabin. I found the kitchen and fully stocked fridge. If his physical didn't arouse me, this kitchen made me want to cook for him. Hell, I was broke and homeless. I *had* to cook for him.

Sausage, cheese grits, smothered potatoes, and a few pancakes later, Teddy found his way downstairs at just the right time.

"Breakfast is ready," I sang as I pointed towards the table.

I was currently making his plate. He watched me happily as I pranced around the kitchen barefoot in my bra and panties.

"Damn, girl. You're pretty *and* you can cook?"

I giggled as I handed him his plate. "I can do a little something. Orange juice or coffee?"

"Coffee would be nice."

The way he looked at me was like he was in awe of me. Funny thing was, being around him didn't give me the insecure feeling that I had felt with Omari or Tre. I know that I had only been around Teddy for a few days, but there was an unusual confident feeling over me. I was not insecure. I did not feel like I had to prove anything. I was confident that he liked me.

Weirdest thing.

I had nibbled as I cooked, so I was no longer hungry. Instead, I continued to nibble as I cleaned the kitchen and started his coffee.

"I gotta run some errands today. You wanna come with me?"

"I could," I answered. I was trying to be nonchalant, but I knew that my broke ass didn't have shit else to do. "I need to go to the motel first and get some clothes."

"You should get *all* of your clothes."

I took a deep breath as I stopped washing the frying pan and looked at him. Sure, I would have loved to be able to hide out in this beautiful home, but I didn't know this nigga. I would have much rather he just gave me some money to stay another week or two in the motel until I figured out how to make some money.

But when I initially saw lust in his eyes the first day that I met him, he now looked more so concerned.

"You don't need to be in that motel. You can stay here."

"You don't even know me. Why do you want a stranger in your house?"

"There is nothing here you can steal. I can totally fuck you up if you try to attack me. I'm not worried," he said with a laugh.

"And you don't have a crazy baby mama or girlfriend that is going to try to fuck me up because I'm staying here?"

I was full of shit. I didn't give a fuck either way.

He laughed again. "No. I told you before. No girlfriend. No baby mama. No nothing." I still wasn't convinced, so he continued to persuade me. "You don't have to sleep in my bed. I'm not on that. I have three other bedrooms. And they're free. It's up to you."

"Hello?"

"What's up, Eboni?"

I hated the way he huffed and puffed like the last thing he wanted to do in the world was waste his time and breathtaking to me.

"Terrance, I need some money. My lights are getting cut off in a few days if I don't pay the bill."

"How much is it?"

"Four hundred."

He smacked his lips. "So you haven't paid the bill in a minute, huh?"

I ignored his sarcasm.

"I ain't got it. I can't help you."

"Terrance, I don't need it all. Anything will help."

"Why I gotta help you pay a bill that you haven't paid in months? And where that nigga at?"

I rolled my eyes into the back of my head. That was always his response, asking where Jamari's father was. He wasn't really helping me financially before. Now he just had what he thought was an excuse.

"I haven't paid that bill because, since you never help me with the kids, I have to use my money towards other things. And wherever 'that nigga' is doesn't matter since my newborn ain't the one leaving lights on all over the house and sucking up all the energy!"

Silence.

"Terrance, please? I can't have my kids in the dark."

Embarrassment caused tears to come to my eyes. I hated to have to ask this bastard for anything. I wished to God that I could work, but sending three kids to daycare would break me. Working would be pointless.

It wasn't supposed to be like this. Every time Terrance knocked me up, I told him that kids were expensive. But he promised me that he would never leave me and that he would always be there for his children.

It was amazingly hurtful how pussy had made him so easily break that promise and leave me out here to fend for our children by myself.

I was listening to him give me excuse after excuse while I could hear my kids making noise inside of Omari's house. So, I hung up on his ass. Asking Terrance for anything was useless, and I had to get my kids before Omari made us leave.

"Tati and Lil' T, what are you doing?!"

As I entered the house, I saw them running through the kitchen chasing a ball.

I heard Omari laughing. He came into the kitchen carrying Jamari. "It's all good. I was playing basketball with them in the living room."

"In the house, Omari?"

"Yea, ma! He got a hoop and er'thang!"

I sighed and shook my head as Lil' T looked at me like I was being a party pooper.

"They're fine," Omari convinced me. "Y'all go head. But not in here. Back in the living room."

I started to follow them, but Omari stopped me. He grabbed my arm gently to get my attention. "Sit down. Let me talk to you."

Discreetly, I rolled my eyes in the back of my head. I didn't want to talk. I was very ashamed of the fact that I had had his baby. I dealt with it by ignoring it. I dealt with it by completely blocking out the kind of friend that I had been to Aeysha by having sex with her man.

I didn't want to talk about anything. I just wanted him to enjoy his son. Period.

"Terrance still not helping you with the kids?"

Thankfully, he wanted to talk about something else. I didn't want to talk about this subject matter either though. I was stressed. Every area of my life caused me complete distress.

Shamefully, I shook my head.

Then he went into his pocket and pulled out some cash. He started counting one hundred dollar bills. When he continued past five hundred dollars, I stopped him.

"Omari, I don't want your money."

I didn't. I had spent months trying to redeem myself after

coercing him out of money like a complete worthless tramp last year.

"I heard you talking to Terrance, and I don't want y'all in the dark."

I fought tears. It was so sad that the man that was supposed to love me and our kids couldn't treat me this way. I had been a total bitch to Omari, and he even had the heart to look out for me.

"Its cool, Omari."

"Let me take care of mine."

"But *yours* didn't run my fucking bill up. Those three in the living room did, and they aren't your responsibility."

Against his will, he didn't fight with me about it. He slid the bills back into his pocket. I think in his heart, he knew where I was coming from. This situation was bogus enough. We had enough guilt to live with. I wasn't willing to add any fuel to the fire.

Deep down inside, I'm sure he wasn't either.

After Detective Howard came to my house, I had a feeling that just maybe Omari had something to do with Aeysha's death. It was way too many coincidences surrounding him and Simone. I figured that after I showed up, he would shun me. I thought that he would keep me away so that he could continue to hide his secret. But after watching him light up every time me and the kids showed up- happy because we filled the room with some sort of reminder of the life he had shared with Aeysha – I knew that he couldn't have had anything to do with killing the love of his life.

Chapter Nine

Gia

"Okay. Who's next?"

"Chance Rogers."

My heart began to beat uncontrollably, knowing that Chance's case was up next. For hours, I sat and heard bail hearing after bail hearing. Some felony cases were credit card fraud or drug cases. Others were murder and rape cases. Many were granted bail. Some weren't. Therefore, I didn't know what to expect.

Within seconds, a door in the back of the courtroom opened. Chance appeared. He was being guided through the courtroom and in front of the judge by a female county sheriff. I tried to catch his eye, but he didn't even hold his head up.

I hadn't been able to talk to him since he was arrested. I drove to the police station the day that he was arrested, but those punk motherfuckers wouldn't even let me talk to him before they shipped him off to the county. I knew that he was able to make phone calls during the day, so I sat by my phone in anticipation of his call.

I never got one.

I was able to call the jail and find out when his bail hearing was. That morning, I was at the county bright and early. After talking to the court clerk, I was told that Chance was given a public defender. I knew that Chance had money saved up, so I wondered why he wouldn't call me to have me hire him a good lawyer that had experience fighting murder charges.

Before court began, I was given the chance to talk to his public defender, but that went nowhere. He didn't know many details about the case and hadn't talked much to Chance. It was like he'd just been given the damn case that morning. I wondered how he would be able to speak for Chance if he didn't even know what the fuck was going on.

"Okay. Let's get started. We have a lot of cases to get through today."

The judge surprisingly seemed interested in every single case. He wasn't the typical asshole authority figure that treated them all like criminals. I hoped that he would see past what Chance was being charged with and at least grant him bail so that he could fight this on the other side of the jail.

"Judge, Mr. Rogers is being charged with the first degree murder of Aeysha Walker and the attempted murder of her infant. She was seven months pregnant at the time of the murder."

The judge couldn't hold back a judgmental smirk as the state's attorney told him Chance's charges. "Thoughts on bail?"

"The defendant has no ties to the state. He was a ward of the state. He doesn't have any family in Chicago. He doesn't have any employment. There is evidence that he was attempting to leave the state a few weeks ago using false identification."

Finally, Chance's public defender spoke up. "Your Honor, the defendant does not have a record. The evidence against Mr. Rogers is circumstantial. There is no concrete evidence connecting him to the victim's murder or to the identity of Reginald Barner…"

"The evidence indeed connects Mr. Rogers to both, Your Honor."

The way the state's attorney dismissed the public defender was embarrassing. I just knew that the public defender would have a rebuttal that insisted that Chance deserved bail, but he said absolutely nothing.

"You all can fight this out during the trial," the judge told them. "As far as the matter of bail, bail is denied. Next case."

I wanted to cry. But just in case Chance actually made eye contact with me, I didn't want my tears to make him feel worse. Yet, he never looked my way. He never even held his head up as the sheriff led him away.

As his public defender waltzed towards me, my heart went out to Chance. I hoped that there was still some fight left in him. During these last two weeks, I saw true remorse for killing Aeysha in him. But despite his guilt, despite the fact that I knew that he'd killed that girl, I just didn't feel like he should be in jail because of it. He'd lived most of his life in jail. He'd done his time.

I met the public defender in the middle of the aisle with

questions. "So what happens next?"

As we walked out of the courtroom, he answered, "There will be a preliminary hearing in about two months."

"What's that?"

"A hearing where the case is assigned to a judge. We could try to get the charges dropped then, but I don't see that happening."

I didn't even hide my dirty look. I didn't like this motherfucker. He didn't have enough fight in him for me. He was just doing his job with no passion.

"How is he doing? Did you tell him that I said to please call me?"

"He is doing how people usually do when they are being charged with murder."

I flinched at his sarcasm. His Black smug ass probably felt like Chance deserved to be in jail. I didn't understand why he was a public defender if he had no heart to defend the motherfucker he was supposed to be defending.

I said goodbye. I didn't need to hear anything else. It was time to go to work. I needed to get my man a real lawyer.

OMARI

I was shocked to see that Aeysha's mother was calling me. After Aeysha's death, we only talked when she wanted to see Dahlia. When she heard that I had moved in with a new girlfriend so soon, she was disgusted.   Aeysha had shared with her mother on many occasions all of the times that she caught me cheating on her, so Mrs. Walker already hated me. Once Aeysha was dead, she completely washed her hands of me. She blamed me and my lifestyle for Aeysha's death.

After Dahlia's death, I never talked to her.

I left Fred and Capone on the porch and stepped into the house to see what she could possibly want.

"Hey, Mrs. Walker…"

Before I could ask her what was up, she went spastic. "You slick son of a bitch! You had my baby killed!"

"Huh?! What are you talking about?!"

"I just left the bail hearing. I talked to the state's attorney…"

"Wait! Hold up! What bail hearing?"

"Chance Rogers! Chance Rogers!"

I had no idea what the fuck she was talking about. Because I was not Aeysha's husband, the police were not obligated to tell me much about the case. I knew that her mother knew way more about what was going on, but she was never friendly enough with me to share that information.

I pleaded with her. I tried to speak as calmly as I could to convince her that I knew nothing and to tell me everything that she knew. But hearing Chance's name had really fucked me up.

"Mrs. Walker, what happened? I don't know anything about Chance being involved in anything."

"I saw that little boy at that house when I came to get Dahlia! You know him, and he killed my baby!"

She was being completely irrational. There was no sense in attempting to get anything out of this woman. She was crying and jabbering nonsense.

"What happened, Omari? You weren't ready for a family? You didn't want Dahlia? You weren't ready to settle down?"

Every question she asked made me sick to my fucking stomach. The fact that she actually thought that I was connected to this shit made me want to punch the fucking wall and her.

"Mrs. Walker, I don't know what you're talking about."

"You know that boy! He's your friend!"

"I didn't meet him until after Aeysha died, Mrs. Walker. I promise."

She hung up on me. I sat in a chair at the kitchen table frozen and staring at the phone. Everything that Mrs. Walker said replayed over and over again like the theme music to an upcoming explosion.

Before I knew it, I was slamming the phone down on the table with so much force that I cracked the screen. I raced towards the front door and barged through it, making the screen door crash against the house as it swung open.

When I saw Capone, it was as if I was a bull that had seen red. I charged towards him. His eyes looked at me with alarm as I flew towards him in anger.

I don't even know how many times I hit him. I punched him in the face so many times that my knuckles felt pain. He tried to fight back. He wrestled with me. But I had caught him off guard and was so much bigger than him that only Fred coming between us had stopped me.

Capone spat through a bloody mouth. "What the fuck is wrong with you?!"

Fred was pulling me off of Capone. I stood reluctantly. I looked at my friend, my brother, my partner. Behind his eyes was emotional pain because I had hurt him. I was in pain because he had crossed me.

"Boss, what's going on?" Fred stood between us, stuck, not knowing who to defend.

"Chance got arrested for killing Aeysha."

Despite leaking blood from his mouth and nose, the news threw Capone for a loop. Fred stood stuck between us.

I looked at Capone with begging eyes. "Tell me you didn't have shit to do with it."

I don't know what pissed him off more– the fact that I hit him or what I had just accused him of.

"The fuck did you just say to me, man?!"

I ignored the fact that he was snarling at me. His anger was irrelevant as fuck. I wanted the truth. "You was working for Ching at the time…"

Capone's shock interrupted me. "C'mon, man…"

"You and Chance went to high school together."

He walked away.

"Man, this is foul," Fred muttered.

I watched Capone as he walked towards his ride, dabbing blood from his wounds that I left on his face.

I was too pissed and confused to think about what I had just done.

Eboni

"Good evening. Thank you for calling ComEd. This is Vanessa speaking. How may I help you?"

"Hi. I have a question about the status of my account."

"What's your name?"

"Eboni Hawkins. Account number 7632834293."

"Give me a few seconds."

I was literally fighting the bubble guts as I rocked Jamari, who was sound asleep in my arms. It was crazy how he was the newborn– expected to cry and drive me crazy– but he was the quietest kid that I had. But no matter how much they got on my last nerve, I loved my kids and wanted the best for them. I did what I had to do to keep them well dressed and groomed. Every toy on their Christmas lists, they got. Everything they asked for on their birthday, they got it. It wasn't their fault that I chose the wrong man to be their father. It wasn't their fault that I didn't make the right choices financially. Therefore, they couldn't suffer on account of me. They weren't going to be in hand-me-downs. They weren't going to starve. They weren't going to sit in the dark, by any means.

I was prepared to grovel for an extension. After selling some food stamps, I had been able to come up with most of the payment that I owed. But I didn't have all of it. ComEd was ruthless, though. They will cut your lights off for being ten dollars past due.

"Ma'am, I have your account up. How may I help you?"

I sighed deeply. This shit was so embarrassing. "My account is scheduled for disconnect and..."

"No, it's not, ma'am."

"Huh?"

"Your account isn't scheduled for disconnect."

"I am looking at the notice. I have a four hundred dollar overdue payment."

"It's been paid, ma'am."

"Huh?!"

The customer service representative laughed at how shocked I was. "Yes, ma'am. It's been paid."

"Are you sure?!"

She giggled at my utter amazement. "Yes, I'm sure, ma'am."

"How?"

"Let me see." I could hear her typing a few keys before she said, "It was paid in cash at a pay station."

I was relieved, but I still felt some kind of way. I knew it was Omari who had paid the bill. Terrance didn't have enough heart or compassion to do such a thing.

"When is the next bill due?"

"You have a credit."

"Credit?!"

"Yes, ma'am. You have a credit of a thousand dollars."

I damn near choked! "What?!"

"Yes, ma'am. It says so right here on the screen."

"Oh... Well, okay. Thank you."

"Is there anything else that I can help you with?"

"No. Thank you."

"No problem. Thank you for calling ComEd. Have a good evening."

I hung up, relieved and in awe. I started to call Omari, but decided against it. I would thank him later. At the moment, I was too fucked up to hold a conversation. I was realizing that after a year, I was still in the position of needing a man to help me. I had done nothing for myself in an entire year. I looked at my kids, huddled around one another watching a movie. I looked down at Jamari sleeping peacefully.

I had to do better for myself than Section 8, food stamps, and begging my way out of disconnect notices. It was time. I thought of Aeysha. Shivers ran down my spine as I thought of the possibilities of leaving this earth before I was able to be who I wanted to be, who I knew that I could be.

I was more than a cute girl with a nice body but no job and nothing to show for myself but four kids.

I had to do it. No matter how much time it took away from my kids, I had to. It was time to stop giving Terrance something to talk about.

SIMONE

I hopped out of Teddy's Range Rover. He let me drive it to make runs. Then I jogged up the stairs of the motel towards my room.

I hadn't been back since leaving two days prior, the day Teddy picked me up and we went to Strokers. He was intent on me not staying there anymore. To ensure that I stayed with him, he took me to the mall yesterday and purchased me a few outfits so that I could run errands with him and do whatever else I might need to do.

I had been honestly having a great time with Teddy. After running errands, he took me sightseeing around Atlanta. We went to the Underground Mall, the World of Coca Cola, and Martin Luther King's childhood home and monument. We dined at five star restaurants. Then he took me to the best greasy spoons with the best fried chicken in the South.

I was able to see him for much more than his potbelly, unimpressive height, and gold fronts. He was a gentleman. It was a breath of fresh air to be around a man that found *me,* and making me happy, his only priority. For once, I wasn't sharing a man. He wasn't hiding me because of a committed relationship or marriage that he was already in. I loved how I had no doubt that, even though we just met, he was all into me and only me.

I hadn't forgotten the task at hand, though. The fact that he liked me made it even cozier for me to hide out in Atlanta. I was forgetting more and more about my life in Chicago, and I prayed that it was forgetting about me.

As I threw my bags in the backseat of the Range Rover, I smiled, thankful that I had been able to get out of Chicago and fall into such a cushy situation.

Yet, the situation didn't stay cushy. As I drove out of the motel, I noticed police lights and sirens a few cars behind me.

I panicked.

I sped up and switched lanes, hoping that it was a random traffic stop for someone else. But as I switched lanes, so did they. That's when I noticed two more squad cars with sirens blaring. Still a few cars behind me, I was able to make a quick left before the light turned red. I was speeding down a residential neighborhood that was dark. As soon as I saw a driveway, I pulled as far into it as I could and turned off the ignition.

I could hear the sirens coming. My eyes darted, attempting to survey the area. I thought about getting out and running. But as soon as my hand grabbed the door handle, the sirens were barreling down the street that I was hiding on. My heart felt as if it was stopping just as squad cars sped by the house that I was sitting in front of.

I sat there paralyzed with fright. I tried to talk myself into thinking that maybe they weren't chasing me. But I knew better. By now, my car had been towed off of the block that I left it on in downtown Chicago. I was sure that investigators figured that I went to the nearby Greyhound station. After looking at the cameras in the station, I was sure that the police were able to see that I had boarded the bus to Atlanta.

My stupid ass had gotten a room at the motel closest to the Greyhound Station in Atlanta. I hadn't used any of my credit cards. However, without the possession of a fake ID, I used my own identification to rent the room.

I fought the onset of a mental breakdown. This shit was real. They were really searching for me.

Atlanta wasn't far enough away or big enough.

I had to keep running.

Chapter Ten

Omari

It had been three days since my altercation with Capone. We hadn't spoken about me putting my hands on him. Though we saw each other at the spots and conducted business as necessary, things were different. There was mad distance. His lip was busted, and his left eye was swollen shut. He had nothing to say to me. That brotherly bond was gone. I could see in his eyes that he felt sorry for me being so lost that I would turn on him so quickly without question.

We were like estranged brothers living under one roof.

I probably should have apologized. But at the time, I still wasn't convinced of his disassociation in Aeysha's murder. Even if he didn't have anything to do with it, the fact that his homeboy from high school was sitting in jail charged for her murder – the same homeboy that Capone brought into in my camp so eagerly– was leaving a bad taste in my mouth.

I didn't know how to tie these loose ends. I was beyond lost. So, that Wednesday morning, I went to the precinct myself for answers. I knew that, since I wasn't Aeysha's next of kin, Detective Howard wouldn't give me any detailed answers. But I figured that I would press my luck anyway.

"Hi, Omari. How are you?"

She walked into the office that I was told to wait in like she didn't have a care in the world. It was crazy how she asked me how I was doing like I wasn't sitting in the middle of the twisted murder of the love of my life.

"Not good," I answered honestly.

She sat behind the desk with a sigh of relief. It was pretty hot in the office. The precinct was old as hell. The air conditioner was a unit sitting in the window. It had to be eighty degrees outside, so it wasn't doing much of a good job of cooling off the room. Detective Howard was sweating under her chin. I was sweating myself, but it was in result of a different type of heat. The summer air was putting me in a fucked up frame of mind. It was reminding me of last summer, the last summer I spent with Aeysha. All the arguing, all the sex, the love, the day that she found out that she was pregnant, began replaying over and over again in my mind. The thoughts were leaving me hot with remorse, guilt, and rage.

"You have some questions for me?"

"Yea, I do," I said eagerly. "I got a weird call from Aeysha's mother the other day. You all have somebody in custody for killing Aeysha? Chance Rogers?"

Detective Howard didn't look too happy to hear that I had as much information as I did.

"Did he really do it? What kind of evidence do you have?"

"I can't tell you that, Omari."

I wasn't surprised. But I kept pressing. "Detective Howard, I would really like to know what's going on."

I wanted to tell her why. I wanted to tell her how I knew Chance. But I didn't want to fuck up my opportunity of taking care of this shit myself.

"Have you seen Simone?"

My head fell into my hands. I couldn't understand why they kept asking me about her. "Me and Simone broke up. I haven't seen her. And why do you keep asking about Simone? Am I a suspect? Because the way Aeysha's mother sounded, she thinks I had something to do with this shit. Like I wasn't ready for a family or some shit, when I did any and everything I had to do to provide for my family. Nah, I wasn't a faithful dude, but I, along with every bitch I fucked with, knew who I loved…"

I bit my lip to stop my outburst. Those words meant nothing to Detective Howard, and I knew it. The police could give a fuck less about emotions and could incriminate me with anything that I said.

"Have a good day, Detective Howard."

I stood up to leave. It was crazy how heavy my heart was. I felt so defeated and lost. I didn't know who to trust, and that confusion was deadly to me and anyone who I imagined may have crossed me.

"Omari." Detective Howard stopped me just as I was reaching for the doorknob. I turned to her in irritation. I was ready to get the fuck up out of there. She hadn't helped me worth shit. Even though I knew my visit was pointless before I even got there, I was let down that a miracle didn't happen.

"Chance Rogers was a ward of the state all of his life. He lived at Lexington House practically since the day he was born."

The way my body reacted was unreal. I had never felt my heart drop to the pit of my stomach so violently. I had never felt my head literally begin to spin so far out of control. The feeling reminded me of how I felt when I watched Aeysha take her last breath and when I held Dahlia's lifeless body.

"There is a triangle around this murder, Omari. You, Simone, and Chance are the connecting the dots. You have an opportunity to come clean right now and give me any information that you have."

Again, I wasn't about to say shit. There was a lot that I wanted to say, tons of questions that I wanted to ask, and a lot that was flowing through my mind. I wasn't thinking straight, and my mind was clouded with the possible deceit of everyone close to me.

Despite the clouds, one thing was clear. Like she said, I was one of the dots connecting everything together.

I stood there looking at her accusing eyes with my hand still on the doorknob. "Am I free to go?"

Oddly, it looked as if Detective Howard found pity in the confusion all over my face. She looked sorry for me. "Sure. You're free to go."

Simone

After a few days, I had talked myself into believing that the police weren't chasing me. Yet, I still had to make a move. Using my own identification at the Greyhound station was a grave mistake. It wouldn't take much for the police to find out where I was. I was sure there was surveillance in the Greyhound station in Atlanta and the motel. I had drawn a direct arrow pointing straight to where I'd run to.

If the police were in fact chasing me that day, they possibly had Teddy's license plate number. It had been three days, and there hadn't been any sign of the police. But the anxiety was fucking killing me.

I had to leave.

"What's wrong, babe?"

Teddy caught me off guard. I was sitting at the kitchen table, staring out into his beautiful backyard, into the trees and beautiful Southern sunshine, drinking a mixture of lemonade and Jack Daniels, from his fully stocked bar. Unfortunately, the Jack Daniels wasn't doing anything to help my anxiety.

"Nothing," I lied, still staring out of the window.

I felt him run his fingers through my hair. "You're lying. You've been acting funny for the last couple of days."

Reluctantly, I turned to face him. He was in Dolce and Gabbana jeans and a plain Versace black tee. I was amazed at the labels that he lounged around the house in on a Wednesday afternoon.

"Sit down. I need to talk to you."

Concern was all over his pudgy brown face as he sat across the table from me. He was into me, so emotionally connected to me, that he immediately reached across the table and held my hand.

When I still sat contemplating, he eagerly asked, "What's up?"

With a deep sigh, I began to orchestrate my lie. "When I went to pick up my things from the motel the other day, there was a note that had been slid under the door. It was from my ex-boyfriend. He found me. He's in Atlanta."

Immediately, Teddy's chest poked out and he got defensive. "Fuck that nigga. I'm not gone let him hurt you!"

"You don't know him, Teddy. He's crazy." My voice began to shake in fear. But not because of the fake abusive ex-boyfriend after me, but because of the very real potential of the police coming to arrest me at any moment. "I think I just… I need to leave. I need to go to another state."

"You're good, girl. How would he find you here?"

"What if he was at the motel the day that I was there? What if he followed me?" I sighed and shook my head. "I don't want to bring this kind of drama into your life. I need to go, at least for a few weeks, to get him off of my scent."

"Where?"

It actually looked like Teddy was contemplating going

wherever I went.

"I don't know. Houston, maybe."

He sat there, silent, as if he were in deep thought. It would have been nice if he came with me. I needed his money.

"Why don't you take a break, a little vacation, and come with me?"

He was satisfied that I'd asked but was hesitant.

"Me and my brother have some business coming up over the next few weeks. I can't leave right now."

I pretended to pout.

"I'm sorry, babe. But I promised him. He really needs my help."

Again, I was staring out of the window, at the trees as they blew freely in the wind. I needed to be one of those trees; freely but discreetly moving about the country. Even if the police weren't chasing me a few days ago, they would soon be on my trail.

"Why do you have this undying devotion to your brother anyway? He doesn't seem like he is very nice to you." That was the most honest I had been during this conversation.

Sure, I was using Teddy. But Jay was a fucking prick. Neither one of us deserved Teddy.

"I know my brother can rub people the wrong way, but deep down inside he is a good dude. After he fucked up last year, I promised to give him another chance and fix our relationship. So that's what I'm doing."

"How did he fuck up?"

"I found out that he slept with Nicey, my ex-fiancé."

He tried, but he couldn't even hide the hurt in his eyes. Right then, I saw why Teddy found it so necessary to prove himself.

"Can you give me a few weeks?" He was begging me. "Just give me a few weeks. I will do whatever I can to make sure that your ex doesn't come near you. After a month, we can go anywhere for as long as you want. I just need to do this for my brother. I can't leave him hanging."

We'll see about that.

Chance

It's funny how being locked up wasn't new for me. It was a lot like being in Lexington House. I was told when to wake up. I was told when to take a shower. I was told when to eat. I was told when to wash my ass.

Once again, and like always, I was a ward of the state.

"Rogers, you have a visitor."

I grimaced to myself as I stood from my cot. No one visited me. After I finally started calling Gia, she constantly begged to be put on my visitation list. I hadn't put her on it yet though. I hadn't been calling her and didn't want visitors because I just wanted to be left alone. So, I knew that my visitor had to be my bullshit public defender.

I was cuffed at the entrance of my cell by a guard. Then that guard took me through the county building. Another guard followed him with his baton in hand, ready to attack if I wanted to act a fool. I wasn't though. Since being locked up, I hadn't resisted any of the process.

I felt like I belonged in jail.

"Mr. Rogers." My public defender greeted me with a bit of a sigh. There was another man in the room with him, along with Detective Howard. "This is state's attorney Terry Woods. You know Detective Howard."

I remained cuffed as I sat across from Detective Howard and

the state's attorney. I peeped how the two guards that led me to the room stood outside of the door, guarding it.

"Long story short, we have an offer on the table, Mr. Rogers."

The way the state's attorney talked to me was so offensive. They didn't give a fuck about me. I was just another case to win.

"For your full testimony against Simone Campbell, we are offering you twenty years with the possibility of parole in fifteen."

My public defender just sat there. The motherfucker didn't even have anything to say, no advice or anything, so I knew that asking him for advice would be hopeless. These motherfuckers were probably cool with each other. They probably had drinks together when they got off work and shit.

I sat at the table with three other people, but I was definitely alone in the room.

"Chance, if you do not take this deal, you can get life in prison," Detective Howard said to persuade me. "If you take this deal, you will at least have a chance to see the light of day when you're thirty-four years old. That's old enough to still get married, have kids, and have a life."

That sounded well and good. However, I had taken the same opportunity that they were offering me away from Aeysha. Like a fool, I'd let my naive dick and greed lead me to kill that chick. I hadn't given her a deal, so I didn't deserve one.

I stood, while saying, "No thanks."

Movement caught the guard's attention. I caught Detective

Howard looking at me like I had nerve. The guards opened the door and quickly grabbed my arms to guide me back to my cell.

This had always been my life. I had always been trapped in a cell alone. I was used to this.

No deal needed.

EBONI

I was feeling really good this particular evening. So when Omari asked me to bring Jamari over, I was happy to. Getting out of the house and getting some fresh air was on my list of things to do anyway.

Over the last few days, I'd done a lot to get the ball rolling into the direction of me providing a better future for myself and my children. The DHS Child Care Assistance Program had finally approved my application. They were paying for daycare and after school care for my oldest three kids. Though working was a priority, school was the most important. I applied at Malcolm X College and was awaiting the approval letter to start prerequisite courses for their radiography tech program in the fall.

Now all I had to do was find a job and a sitter for Jamari.

Things were looking up, and I was so excited about it. But when I walked pass Fred and into Omari's trap house, I saw that Omari clearly was not wearing a smile on his face like I was.

"Hey, Eboni," he said nonchalantly as he took Jamari out of my arms. He looked behind me, confused. "Where the rest of the kids?"

"With my mama," I answered as I looked at him with concern. He reeked of tequila and his whole aura was just fucked up. "You okay?"

"Yeah, I'm good," he lied as he walked into the living room.

I followed close behind. I could tell that he was tipsy. If his drunk ass dropped my baby, Detective Howard was going to be after me for murder next.

"Omari, he's sleep. I don't like people to hold him while he's sleep. He'll get spoiled. Is there somewhere I can lie him down?"

"Yea, c'mon."

We turned around, went back down the hall, and entered a room off of the kitchen. I was surprised to see that it was a baby bed set up inside. Eerily, I noticed the baby decorations on the walls and realized that it was Dahlia's old room.

Watching him lay Jamari down was so heartwarming. The way that he ran his fingers through Jamari's curly hair was so loving. It reminded me of how loving Terrance was when I had Lil' T, when he was in love with our children and in love with me.

"You want a drink?"

I answered, "Yes," before I knew it. Just that quick, my good mood was overshadowed by the usual sadness and insecurity that Terrance casts over my life like an approaching thunderstorm.

Back in the kitchen, he poured 1800 and lime juice into a red plastic cup. Though he probably didn't need one, he poured himself another as well.

Three drinks in, I was leaning on the couch, barefoot and rubbing my toes into the carpet. Omari's body weight was leaning against me. He had been unusually quiet all day. I wondered why in the hell he asked me to come over in the first place.

"I think I should go, Omari. It's getting late and I'm tipsy."

He looked at me like I was crazy. "You ain't driving my baby home tipsy."

I laughed as I stood up. "Boy, I can drive. I'm good."

Before I knew it, he'd stood and grabbed my waist with so much force that I initially got scared. But the look in his eyes made the fear go away.

He asked me, "What I say?"

The way he stared into my eyes made me weak in the knees. I could ignore the past and the bullshit that we'd done all I wanted to, but one could never deny the sex appeal that oozed from this man.

I was stuck, literally. I couldn't even shy away from his stare. Still looking me in the eyes, he pulled me by the waist closer to him. The tequila had me feeling some kinda way. But apparently it had Omari feeling quite froggish because he kissed me as if he'd just made love to me the night before. He was drunk– *very*. And I was horny– *very*. He was the last person that I had sex with over nine months ago. It had been a few weeks since I had my baby, and my pussy was not allowing me to continue down the positive path that I was on when I walked in that house a few hours prior.

He continued to kiss me as he guided me into the nearby bedroom. He closed and locked the door while taking off his shirt. His back was a work of God. He turned around. The sight of the dark chocolate chiseled chest and arms confirmed that there indeed was a God.

"Take this shit off," he moaned as he tugged at my shorts.

When I didn't move fast enough, he walked up on me, his sexually masculine body taking my breath away. He began to kiss me again, as his hands pulled my shorts down to my ankles. When he pushed me down on the bed, I knew that this meant nothing. I knew that this sex was going to mean nothing to him in the morning. But, at the moment, I wanted nothing more than that dick in me.

He lifted each foot and pulled my leg through the shorts. Once my legs were able to move about the bed, he spread them apart and lost his face in between my thighs. I sat up on my elbows. The sight of his beautiful dark arms, wrapped so firmly around my thighs that his muscles flexed, made me leak sweet juices into his mouth.

I came so immaturely, like a virgin. He sat up with a satisfied grin and the evidence of his meal all over his face. He reached toward the windowsill. I wondered for what until I saw the condom.

It was crazy how, prior to that moment, I had not one sexual thought of Omari. I only wanted him to know his son. But looking at his dick in his hands gave me raunchy and lustful thoughts of all kinds of possibilities. The smile on his face was cute and devilish. He climbed on top of me with confidence. He knew that he could fuck like a beast. I feared my ability to think straight after this fuck session. But as soon as I felt the dick inside of me, my fear flew out of the window that was inches away from me.

He rode me like such a professional. I remembered the nights that I lay in bed, pregnant and alone, full of guilt because all that I could do was think of the days and nights that he was on top of me, fucking me into all kinds of ratchet behavior.

He lay on top of me, our chests hugging one another's, his mouth to my ear whispering all kinds of nasty, inappropriate, slutty shit into my ear. My eyes rolled into the back of my head as his dick penetrated my pussy ever so miraculously.

I was in a daze as orgasm after orgasm fell from me.

"Yea. Cum all over this dick."

I was transfixed.

"Damn. This pussy good."

I was confused.

"You cumin' again, ain't you? C'mon, baby."

I was lost.

Before the dick, I had my shit together. I had goals, dreams, and aspirations. But after the dick, I was lost, turned out all over again, and needed Iyanla to fix my life.

OMARI

After we both bust a nut, Eboni got out of the bed so fast that my eyes were closing before I could ask her where she was going.

I woke up in the bed shirtless with my pants still unzipped. I was groggy from the nut I busted and the leftover effect of the massive amount of tequila that I'd drank in such a short amount of time.

I hadn't been able to process what Aeysha's mother told me, or what Detective Howard had laid on me. I was going through so many scenarios in my head that the shit was wigging me out. The only thing I could do to calm down was drink.

I fumbled into the dark living room. When I flipped the light switch, Capone made a sudden movement on the couch.

"Man, what the fuck," he mumbled.

Instantly, I got angry. "Shut the fuck up, nigga!"

I didn't know who the fuck to believe. I knew this was my nigga. I knew this had been my right hand without no question for some time. But somewhere in my circle of supposed loyal "fam" was a dirty motherfucker. The accusations were pointing at everybody. I wanted it *not* to be whoever the blame was being put on.

"Fuck you say, my nigga?!" Capone hopped up from the couch, pulling up his jeans along the way.

I had never seen him so angry. I had never been so angry. We were like savages, when once we were like brothers.

I think our anger was so escalated because there was a lot of hurt and confusion between us.

When he charged at me, I charged back. Honestly, I didn't want to fight him. I was just mad. I was mad that Aeysha wasn't there. I was mad that I still cried over her death. I was mad that I wasn't over it. I was pissed that I knew that somebody around me had something to do with it, but I didn't know who and I didn't know why. Thoughts of Dahlia's death set me beyond furious.

We hit each other like we didn't even know each other; wrestled each other into submission like we hadn't broke major bread together.

Tables knocked over.

Lamps shattered.

Glass broke. I could feel pieces of it as it sliced my skin while we wrestled on the floor.

"Is y'all serious, man?! What the fuck?!"

I could hear Fred. He was somewhere in the room. I couldn't see him. Capone and I were on the ground. We were holding each other. He held me around my neck while I held him around his.

Fred tried to separate us but his hands felt like a child's. The more he attempted to pull us apart, the tighter we held on.

After a few seconds of stubbornness, I heard Capone mutter, "Fuck this shit," before letting me go with a jolt that snapped my neck back. I didn't even bother reacting. Now that the smoke had cleared, I felt like a fool.

Lying on the floor watching two young guys look down on me like they were disgusted with me should have given me some feeling of shame. But it didn't. I stood from the floor in a hurry and left, knocking the flat screen down and shattering it along the way.

Chapter Eleven

Gia

It had been a little over two weeks since Chance was locked up. I had been twerking my ass off at Sunset to come up with ten grand. Finally, I had enough money to meet with the lawyers suggested to me by Asia. She was a stripper at Sunset as well. She was also one of the only chicks I trusted up in there. We talked outside of work sometimes, so I knew that her man was also fighting a murder case. She referred me to his lawyers.

I was so nervous as I approached the office building on Washington Boulevard downtown. Chance's public defender hadn't been any help whatsoever. He rarely answered my calls. When we finally talked, he wasn't any help. There weren't many details about Chance's case that I was privy to anyway, since I wasn't his wife or next of kin.

As I rang the bell, memories of the last days I spent with Chance were flooding my brain. It was crazy how much I missed his young ass. I was so eager to get him out of jail, not only because I gave them the evidence to arrest him, but also because I desperately wanted my man back. My days weren't the same without him.

The voice over the intercom brought me out of my gloomy

thoughts. "May I help you?"

"I'm here to see Mr. Peter Coulis."

"What is your name?"

"Gianna Michaels."

The door buzzed. I opened it and walked in with so much hope.

The receptionist gave me some standard forms to fill out and told me to have a seat. I was only half way done filling them out when a tall older white man came out of one of the offices.

"Sorry to keep you waiting, Gianna. Hi. I'm Peter."

I stood and shook his hand. "Hi. Please call me Gia."

"Nice to meet you, Gia, though under unfortunate circumstances. Follow me."

I followed him into a nearby office. He was carrying a file folder under his arm. I assumed that it was a file on Chance's case.

"Have a seat. Do you want some water or tea?"

"No, thank you."

Admittedly, I was intimidated. This, murder and love, was a new experience for me.

"Okay, so let's get to it, Gia. As you know, there isn't much that I can legally tell you but, after reading over his file, I think Chance has a chance with us."

My heart filled with glee. "Really?"

Peter sucked his teeth as if it was obvious. "The state's evidence is weak."

"Well, how did they arrest him?"

"Unfortunately, people get arrested with weak evidence all the time."

"So when you say that he has a chance, what do you mean?"

"Well, what I am going to do is attempt to get the charges dropped during the preliminary hearing next month. Like I said, this evidence is weak. There is no concrete evidence connecting him to this murder. No gun. No DNA. No eyewitnesses. It's all circumstantial, at best."

"And if they don't drop the charges?" I wanted to be optimistic, but I also did not want to give myself or Chance false hope.

"We'll have to fight it out in a trial. I can attempt to ask for another bail hearing. Cases can take years. He shouldn't have to sit in jail for that long with this type of evidence."

He sighed sympathetically as I looked at him. He was reading the fear in my face, despite the fact that he was promising me a positive change of events.

"I'm sorry," I said, apologizing for my apparent apprehension. "I appreciate you taking his case. I just don't know what to believe anymore. I'm literally scared to think positive."

"Gia, I have had some real criminals sitting at this table. I have had to defend murders with DNA traces that were a mile long. Chance is going to be okay…"

"But he's in jail."

"And unfortunately it is very easy for someone to get arrested on a bullshit charge. But that is why you pay us to fight the case. You just have to be patient, okay?"

That was easier said than done. I went spastic and put my man in jail like a fucking idiot. Patience was not a virtue. It was driving me fucking crazy. Every day he stayed in there, I was wasting away and so was he.

SIMONE

For two weeks, I had been living my life on pins and needles. I left Chicago to flee from this feeling of being chased but, like a dumb ass, I made it so that I could still easily be found.

I had to get the hell out of Georgia. Every time a cop car appeared, my heart stopped. Every time I heard sirens, my heart stopped. My blood pressure was out of control with anxiety. I was either going to get arrested or stroke out from the stress.

But I couldn't go anywhere. I literally had a hundred dollars to my name. Teddy was so far up my ass that I couldn't even rummage through his shit to see if he had a stash somewhere. But, despite his outer appearance, his money was legit. It was stashed in Chase accounts, not floorboards, as I was use to.

When I heard the alarm chirp, I figured that Teddy was home from running to the bank. So I got out of bed, slipped on a pair of leggings and a tee, and trotted down stairs.

However, it wasn't Teddy coming through the door. To my surprise, it was his brother, Jay. It sickened me that these two were so close that Jay had a key to his brother's home. No matter how good Jay looked, his insides were ugly as fuck. I did not like the way that Teddy felt so inferior to him that he literally made himself look like a fool to seem as good as Jay. Jay was around enough for me to realize that he was a complete asshole to Teddy. He mocked him. He thought so highly of himself that he had no issue staring at me and giving me flirtatious eyes behind Teddy's back.

He was such a fucking creep.

"Hey, Jay," I spoke, attempting to smile as convincingly as possible as we met at the bottom of the steps. "Teddy isn't upstairs. He'll be here in minute though."

Usually when Jay would flirt with me, I acted like I didn't see it. But as he glided towards me licking his lips, I smiled flirtatiously, inviting him in.

"I know," he told me as he smiled seductively. He walked towards me, cornering me between the wall and the rail of the stairway. "I just got off the phone with him."

I challenged him, not backing away as he came closer and closer. If the contour of his arms and exposed chest through his wife beater wasn't captivating enough, his Dolce and Gabbana was choking me with lust.

"Something you need?"

He was so close to me that I could feel his heart beating. Biting his lip erotically, he looked me up and down– from my high messy bun, to my tank, leggings, and bare hot pink painted toes.

"Need *and* want," he finally answered.

My eyes approved his flirtation and gave him the green light. He groped my breast, squeezing my nipples between two fingers, and a soft deep groan left his full pretty lips. His hands then left my breasts, and traced the outline of my coke bottle shape until they landed on my ass.

"Damn, girl. My brotha know what to do with all this?"

"He does a pretty good job."

"I can do better."

Just I suspected, out of the corner of my eyes, I saw Teddy pulling up in his Range Rover.

"You think so, huh?" I grabbed his hardened dick through the basketball shorts that he was wearing. Figures that his cocky ass wasn't even packing. He had an above average attitude with an average sized dick.

Fuck this nigga.

"What you gone do with that?" His face was in my neck, so he couldn't see Teddy approaching the house. But I knew that once he was close enough, Teddy could see us through the glass panes surrounding the front door.

I moaned sexually. "What do you want me to do with it?"

"Anything you want, sexy."

Just as he responded, I began to yell, scream, and flail my arms. "Get the fuck off of me!"

Instantly, that got Teddy's attention and he frantically went for his keys as he ran towards the front door.

Jay looked at me like I was crazy. "What the fuck yo'?!"

"Get away from me! What is wrong with you?!"

Jay looked at me like he was terribly confused as he attempted to block my blows.

"You nasty motherfucka! What you think I am?! Some type of

hoe?!"

Still confusion consumed him. As Teddy barged through the front door, Jay's chest lowered in regret and embarrassment.

Teddy ran towards me with his chest heaving. "What the fuck is going on, babe?!"

"Your punk ass brother came on to me! He was grabbing me and shit!"

Jay was so shocked at my response that he laughed. "Man, are you serious?"

"You was trying to take some pussy, nasty motherfucka!"

When he laughed, Teddy responded like I never thought he would. He charged at Jay. Upon impact they began wrestling and fist fighting. Jay, being drastically taller than Teddy, had an advantage. He flung Teddy around on the stairway with ease.

"Stop! Get the fuck off him!" I pulled at Jay's shirt, attempting to get him off of Teddy, who was underneath him on the stairs attempting to punch and kick his way free.

"Get the fuck off me, bitch!" Jay reached back and pushed me away from him. With his attention on me, he let Teddy go. "You lyin' ass bitch. Teddy, what the fuck, man? You gone listen to this bitch ova me..."

I shrieked, "I ain't gone be too many more bitches!"

Teddy stood up with rage all over his face. "Get the fuck out my house, bro!"

Jay was hurt. "Are you serious? You been knowing this bitch

not even a month. The pussy that good you can't see the truth? She was throwing me the pussy, man."

"Just like Nicey was throwing you the pussy?"

Jay's face filled with so much guilt that he couldn't even look at Teddy.

"Get the fuck out. Step!"

"For real, bro? I was foul with Nicey, but this bitch here is lyin'. I wasn't trying to take shit. She wanted it."

Teddy flexed with anger. They were now chest to chest. Jay couldn't hide the humor he found in Teddy's rage.

Jay sucked his teeth. He looked at Teddy like he had lost his mind. He scolded at me like I was the worst bitch in the world. "Fuck both of y'all. I'm out."

OMARI

Eboni hadn't been over since we had sex. For two weeks, she rarely answered my calls. When she would answer, she made excuses for why she had to get off the phone. She barely responded to my text messages.

That day, she was giving me the same attitude.

"Hey, Omari. What's up?"

"I thought you were bringing Jamari over yesterday."

She couldn't even lie straight. "My mother couldn't watch the other kids."

"You could have brought them with you."

She smacked her lips. "I don't want to keep bringing my babies over to that trap house, Omari."

Sighing, I told her, "I'm getting a crib in a few weeks. Just be a little patient with me. But you know I wanna spend as much time with Jamari as I can."

She ignored me. I could hear her kids laughing and playing in the background.

"You home?"

"Yea."

"Well, I'm coming over there."

She sighed in frustration. I knew that would fuck with her. She couldn't give me any excuses now.

"Omari, you don't have to do that. I know you don't want to

come over here."

I really didn't. But at a time like this, I just really didn't want to be alone. Being in the company of block boys was still like being alone emotionally, especially since they were all looking at me like I was crazy. They were walking on eggshells around me. I needed to be around family. I needed to be around somebody that understood.

"It's okay. I'll be okay," I promised her. "I'm on my way."

When she didn't say no, I hung up, hopped off the couch, and got the hell out of the house. So many things were on my mind that it had been hard for me to think straight. Along with Eboni treating me funny, Aeysha's mother wouldn't answer my calls. I'd been hearing through mutual friends that her family was convinced that I had something to do with Aeysha's murder. I'd even gotten a few threatening messages in my Facebook inbox. There were so many unanswered questions. Since Detective Howard was treating me like a suspect too, wasn't shit that I could do. Racking my brain was the only option, but that shit was driving me crazy.

I was at Eboni's crib within fifteen minutes. Just turning onto the block made my stomach ball up into knots. I drove towards the house, looking for a close parking spot. As I did, I drove by the spot where Aeysha's body laid. I stared at the spot, while all the possibilities of what really happened to her bounced around in my head.

Then I kept driving. I drove past the old apartment building before I accidently lay my eyes on it. It frustrated me that after a year, I was still hurting and lost. I really wanted to be at a place where I thought of Aeysha and smiled. I desperately wanted to be at a place where I could relax into her memory like a summer day.

But that wasn't going to happen until the reason that she passed was at rest and I knew that it had nothing to do with me.

Chapter Twelve

Chance

Last week, I finally filled out the necessary paperwork for Gia to get on the visitation list. So, that day, I walked into the visitation room and laid my eyes on an eagerly awaiting Gia. She looked good– damn good. She was a sight for my sore eyes, I swear to God.

She dressed like she wanted me to be impressed. I definitely was. But I couldn't even enjoy it. She was in a pair of damaged jeans, crop top, and heels. But I was in a fucking orange jump suit.

Despite having to see me in this cold and dark room, she had the brightest most beautiful smile on her face.

"Hey, baby."

There was minimal contact allowed, so I could only hug her. I had to fight the urge to hold her close to me, take in her flowery smell, and squeeze her booty.

I barely said, "What's up," as we sat across from one another at the table. Other inmates were inches away from us. Their mates or families were inches away from Gia.

"You tell me."

"Why don't *you* tell *me*? I got a visit from a lawyer this morning. You hired me another lawyer?"

I couldn't believe it when I was called out of my cell. I thought the state's attorney was there to hound me, yet again. Surprising, three suits were waiting on me with a folder five inches thick, full of paperwork pertaining to my case.

Gia looked shocked to see that I wasn't as excited about this as she looked. "Yea. I did."

"Why?"

"What do you mean why?!" She realized that she was getting loud. She looked nervously at the guards and then lowered her tone. "Because your lawyer sucked. He wasn't even fighting for you."

"What's there to fight for, Gia? I'm guilty."

Immediately, she leaned in and whispered, "Don't you ever say that again."

"Gia, this ain't no petty weed charge. This shit is serious."

"And they have very little evidence, Chance."

Gia looked so eager. She was so willing to fight. I wished that I felt that way. I wished that I gave a fuck. I didn't though. I had been running from this shit for a year. It was time to face my punishment. I killed that girl. No jury, no judge, no evidence needed.

I killed her, and I should pay for it.

It was like Gia was reading my mind. She stared into my eyes. I know that to her they looked weak and tired. "Don't give up, Chance. Please don't give up."

"This isn't your fight, Gia."

"But it's yours. And since you aren't fighting, let me and the lawyers fight for you."

I looked away from her begging eyes because I couldn't take it anymore. I didn't want to fight this out. I just wanted to be left alone. I looked around at the other inmates, men that I had spent the last few weeks living with. Like me, some of them were guilty. But some of them were innocent.

"They don't have any evidence. No weapon. No vehicle. No proof. None, Chance. The lawyer said that he has a chance to get this dropped at your preliminary hearing."

That should have brought joy to my heart. It only made me feel worse though. I was stuck between the desire to live the rest of my life as a free but guilt-stricken man or to live the rest of my life behind bars. In either case, I would be racked with the same guilt.

EBONI

When Omari opened the door, he looked shocked to see me and a porch full of kids.

"Hey." I barely spoke to him. I didn't want to be there but after seeing him drive by the building the day before, I felt so sorry for him.

"What's up?"

Immediately, I handed Jamari to him. I told Lil' T to keep an eye on his sisters while they played jump rope with the rope that they brought with them. Then I followed Omari into the house.

"Thank you," Omari told me with eyes full of relief.

The fact that Omari felt the need to even thank me made my heart heavy with guilt as we walked through the house. I knew that he wanted desperately to see his baby over the past two weeks, but I just couldn't bring myself to come back over here.

Having sex with Omari was all kinds of wrong– all kinds! Don't get me wrong. It was good – so good – damn good! The gates of heaven opened. I heard birds chirping. I heard an angelic choir singing!

Whew!

And that is why he and I could never ever *ever* have sex again. I didn't want to be that person anymore; no matter how good the dick was.

I was on a great path of making things better for myself and my tribe of kids. I couldn't afford to adopt any unnecessary bad karma.

And I believe that Omari knew that and that is why, despite knowing that I have been giving him the cold shoulder since I last saw him, he didn't even mention it.

As we got comfortable on the couch, Jamari began to coo. Omari looked like it was the best thing he had heard in forever. Jamari had gotten so big over the last few weeks. More and more features of Omari were emerging. It was miraculous how much they looked alike.

"Omari, Aeysha's mother called me last night."

She had. That was another reason why I came to see Omari. Things were getting so crazy with Aeysha's case.

I caught Omari sighing inwardly. "What did she say?"

"She mentioned one of your friends being charged with Aeysha's murder a few weeks ago."

"One of my friends, huh?"

"Yea. Some guy named Chance."

"I know about it."

"Apparently, her whole family does too. But when she told me that you had to have something to do with it, I told her that she was crazy."

Surprisingly, he looked relieved that I would take up for him.

"She tried to say that you weren't ready for a baby. She said that you was always cheating on Aeysha and that you just wanted out. I told her that that was the farthest thing from the truth. I told her that, even if she is Aeysha's mother, I saw you guys every damn day. I know that you wanted nothing else but that baby and Aeysha."

I guess my genuine belief in his innocence had a major effect on him. He laughed a little as he wiped a lonely tear that rolled down his face.

"What's funny?"

"I'm sick of crying. I feel like such a bitch."

"Any man that doesn't cry about losing his woman and daughter is a bitch."

Taking a deep sigh, attempting to get himself together, he asked, "Did Aeysha's mother say anything else?"

"No."

"So Chance is the only suspect?"

I shrugged my shoulders. "I don't know. I guess. Have you heard anything?"

He slightly shook his head and just answered, "Nah."

This topic of conversation was obviously bringing him down, so I changed the subject. "Did you pay my light bill?"

His grin was filled with guilt. "I don't know what you're talking about."

Playfully, I smacked his leg. Gosh, his dick was so big that even though I smacked his thigh, it brushed against my hand. His eyebrow rose with guilt. The way his eyes twinkled with charm drove me crazy. But I shook it off. "Why did you pay my bill?"

"I don't know what you're talking about."

"Omari, I don't need your help."

"You needed Terrance's."

"Those are his kids. He is supposed to help me."

"But Jamari is my child too. I know you might feel too guilty to admit it, but he's mine. And I'm always gonna help mine. And there is nothing you can do to stop me... as you can see."

I could only grimace. He was right.

"What are you going to do, Eboni?"

It was a vague question, but I knew what he meant. He was referring to my life, and asking how I was going to take care of myself and my children. I was still in the impoverished state that I was in when he moved out.

"I got accepted into Malcolm X."

His eyes brightened. "You did?! That's what's up."

I smiled. "Thanks. I've been looking for a job. I finally got some assistance for day care. Now all I have to do is find somebody that I trust to watch Jamari."

"I'll do it."

"Are you crazy, Omari? I do not want my baby at no trap house all day."

"I'll pay Paula to do it."

"I do not want no hype watching my baby!"

"True, true," he said with a chuckle. "We'll figure something out."

"We'll?"

"Yes, *we*. I know you aren't used to it, but I want to be as involved in his life as I can. Even if Jamari wasn't here, you and your kids are like family to me. You are the only person, besides my mother, that I can sit and reminisce with about Aeysha and Dahlia. You and my mother are the only people that understand my hurt. Being around you and the kids remind me of the family that I lost. You make me feel like they are still here."

SIMONE

I knew that if Teddy got mad at Jay that he would spend every waking moment with me. For two weeks, we had been inseparable. We spent most of our time in the house, since that is where he conducted most of his business. We spent many late nights in Atlanta partying, drinking, and spending a lot of cash.

He kept me close. He wanted to ensure that my abusive ex wouldn't find me. Every now and then I would freak out and pretend that I saw him in a crowd, or pretend as if I saw his car following us.

I was comfortable in Atlanta– quite comfortable. But I was still anxious that I would be found. That anxiety rose as I sat in Teddy's beautiful tub soaking in a bubble bath and scrolling through the Chicago news on his iPad.

Frightening headlines scared me so much that I damn near dropped the iPad in the hot sudsy water.

The headlines read, "Chance Rogers arrested for the murder of Aeysha Walker".

It was a small article in the Metro section of the Chicago Sun Times. I would have overlooked it had the names not rang such horrifying bells. Instantly, I began to shed tears. At first, being charged with this murder was all possibilities. Everything was suspect and circumstantial. I was running from maybes and what ifs. But reading that article put a definite dread of capture in the pit of my stomach.

They had Chance.

I was next.

I continued to read the article, searching for clues of what evidence they had. Yet, the article only stated that he had been arrested and was not given bail. It went on to say that the police were searching for another suspect.

I shut down the iPad and sat it on the floor next the tub. I began to wail. I was too scared to even hide my cries or my tears. I was so scared that I was literally shaking. I wanted to get out of the tub, but my legs felt like noodles.

"Babe?"

I didn't even bother hiding my tears as I heard Teddy coming into the bathroom. I had been able to fake my way through this when this all was circumstantial. Now I thought back to the day that I thought the police were chasing me and figured that they most definitely were. I felt like a mouse in a maze with no way out. At every entrance of this maze were the police ready to arrest me.

"What's wrong, babe?"

Every time that he called me babe, my tears and cries became worse. He sat on the ledge in front of the tub, reached over, and hugged me. The water that dripped from my arms and hands drenched his Versace tee shirt.

"It's going to be okay."

It wasn't. There I was in a beautiful home with a man that had no problem accepting me and loving me unconditionally. I had stooped so low in an attempt to get this same love and acceptance from another man that I had killed a woman and her baby. I *killed* them. And now I would be locked up, away from any man and any opportunity to receive the love that I killed for.

"Babe, talk to me."

"I'm scared," was all that I could say. He thought that I was scared of my make believe ex; scared that he would take my life. I was certainly scared of my life being taken away. So his assumptions were right to a certain extent.

"You don't have to be afraid. I'm here for you. I'll never let him hurt you again. I love you."

He wasn't my physical type. I looked at him and not one drop of lustful moisture rose to the surface of my skin. But hearing him say those words only made me feel ten times worse.

All my life I'd waited to hear those three words from a man that I did not have to borrow or steal.

Chapter Thirteen

Simone

The next morning, I woke up to the smell of sausage, pancakes and eggs. I felt drunk. All evening I'd silently cried myself to sleep, wondering where the hell I was going to run to and how the hell I was going to get there with not a dollar to my name. I was heavy with worry, headache, and fear.

I still had maybe a hundred dollars in cash that I kept for the day that I might need it. Teddy had purchased so many outfits, shoes, and purses for me that many of them still had tags on them. I lay biting my nails all night wondering how I could take them back without a receipt for the cash refund.

I wanted to feel like the level of desperation that I'd reached was at an all time low. But the realization that my lowest point was what had put me in this position jolted me out of bed.

Never a woman to allow myself to lose, I slipped on a pair of shorts and left the bedroom. I had to get out of this funk and figure out how in the hell I was going to get out of town.

As I walked into the kitchen, I spotted Teddy bopping happily to some 2 Chainz that was playing on the stereo in the adjoining den. I spotted the kitchen knives displayed decoratively on the granite island. I actually thought of taking the largest one, putting it to his throat, and demanding that he drive to the nearest ATM and give me everything that the daily limit would allow. But I quickly pushed away that hasty thought. He was a small man, but still a man. He would possibly be able to whoop my ass and take the fucking knife from me.

Still I thought of what I could do. I looked around the kitchen and den at things I could possibly pawn for a couple hundred dollars– just enough to get me to another state.

Then, he did something that was better than any of the erratic thoughts that I was having.

"Sit down," he told me as he took me by the hand.

He guided me to the table. As I sat, he handed me the champagne glass in his hand. I assumed that it was a Mimosa. Then he sat beside me, lovingly placing his hand on my thigh.

"You know when I told you that I loved you last night, I meant it, don't you?"

I gulped down the Mimosa, barely listening to him. I was still speculating what to steal and how to get it to the nearest pawn shop.

Yet, I managed to nod in response.

"Would you think I was crazy if I wanted to marry you?"

Before I knew it, I laughed aloud and answered, "Hell yea."

He was dead serious as he looked at me. There wasn't a glimpse of his gold fronts because he was not wearing a smirk or smile. To spare his feelings, I stopped laughing and took him seriously. "Are you being for real?"

"Yea. I mean, I know it's only been like two months, but I know that I love you. I've never met a woman like you. And I want to marry you."

What he meant was that he'd never had a woman that looked like me. He'd never had a woman with an ass like mine who he thought liked him genuinely. He'd never had a woman like me, and every day he could see that I was closer and closer to running.

Over the weeks I'd grown to like the man on the inside way more than I could like his outer appearance. But I didn't love him. Nor did I ever want to marry him.

But I smiled, because marriage was the answer to all the questions that kept me awake last night.

"I'd love to," I said with fake happiness that brought tears to my eyes. They were real tears though. I was just that happy that luck had come in the nick of time once again.

He sighed happily. He took my hand and kissed it. His doe eyes twinkled. He was the happiest little man in the world.

"But I don't know," I said letting him down. "I mean, I don't have a job. I don't have money. I totally depend on you. I wouldn't feel right. It's like I'm living off of you. This is what happened with my ex. I want my own." I looked at him with fake sadness and worry in my eyes. But in the back of my mind, I hoped he was getting the hint.

"Baby, I got you. Money is nothing. I'll give you your own

account, if that is what makes you feel comfortable. Just marry me, please."

My insides relaxed and turned into a feeling of happiness.

He sounded absolutely crazy. Yet, marrying him was crazy enough to be exactly what I needed.

OMARI

It was only about two in the afternoon, but I'd had enough Patron for the effects to last me all day. I wasn't sloppy drunk. I was just tipsy enough that I didn't feel the constant worry headache, the consistent heavy heart, or that gut feeling in my stomach.

I was just sitting there on the couch at the trap in Riverdale looking at the television like I gave a fuck about the ghetto ass bitches on Maury getting paternity tests for their kids.

Luckily, Eboni was on the way with Jamari. I was so appreciative of her. If it wasn't for her– if it wasn't for Jamari– I just didn't know how I would get through the day.

Capone caught my eye as he walked into the living room. Motherfucker had the nerve not to say shit to me as he went into the spare bedroom. I was sure he was going into one of the stash spots for something.

Shit was so weird between us. After our second fight, we'd just become more estranged. We conducted business like we didn't even know each other. I was too confused to actually apologize. He was way too ornery to give me the benefit of the doubt.

But even under the influence, I knew that I was wrong for how I'd been stepping to my fam. So, when I saw him leaving the bedroom out of the corner of my eye, I stood to confront him. I didn't know what I was going to say. I knew that there was nothing that I could say to really make up for the stunts I'd pulled. But when he flexed and squared up like he was about to hit me, my heart broke– real talk.

"Fam..."

Biting words cut me off. "Fam we ain't, my nigga."

"Bro, I been goin' through some shit," I tried to explain.

As I walked towards him, he walked away.

"Fuck you, nigga."

He cut his eyes at me so hard that I stood back.

I couldn't blame him.

I couldn't knock him for how he dismissed me. I couldn't blame him for turning his back on me and walking out. But I could definitely blame myself for being guilty of losing another family member.

Just as I slumped back down on the couch and grabbed my cup, I heard footsteps coming back into the living room. I looked up, hoping that it was Capone. I needed to fix this shit. It was obvious that he was done with me. I wondered since we were still breaking bread together what he planned to do. Street niggas were ruthless when they felt violated. Since he had access to every ounce, brick, and stash of cash, his possible retaliation put all kinds of thoughts in my head.

But it wasn't him coming into the living room. It was Eboni. She was a pretty sight too. No matter the grief and conspiracy surrounding me, I couldn't deny how fine she was. The baby weight was falling off her like melting snow. She was once again the pretty girl with a body like the baddest stripper in King of Diamonds.

"Where's the kids?"

"Summer camp!" I don't think I'd ever seen a smile on her so bright. "Finally got the money from the state to send they asses to camp. And I laid Jamari down in the room on my way in. He's sleep."

Lust took over me as she sat next to me. It had to be some kinda illegal for her to wear shorts so little with an ass like that. Obviously she was excited about her stomach being flat again, because she was wearing a sleeveless button up shirt that tied up at the navel. Simone always wore expensive labels. Chanel this. Celine that. I knew that Eboni couldn't afford those kinda labels. Aeysha never could either. But it was crazy how their basic labels from Forever 21 looked so much better on them than any pair of True Religion or Gucci on Simone.

"Omari," she said with a warning tone as she caught me looking her juicy thighs up and down. "Stop it."

Her legs were so moisturized that they looked damn near thirst quenching.

I reached to touch the smoothness of her brown skin, but she gently pushed my hand away.

"Stop, Omari."

I knew that she really didn't want me to. Her mouth was saying no, but her eyes were begging for my touch. Her pussy was so phat through the denim of her shorts that I could swear it was reaching out to me.

"I'm serious," she said, reading my eyes and scooting away from me. "We can't do that anymore."

"Why not?" My pout was real. My dick was so sad to hear that.

"Because it ain't right! You're just using me."

"That's harsh."

"You are. You're drunk. Just like the last time you tried it."

"Drunk mind speaks a sober truth."

"You're going through a lot. And you ain't gon' take it out on my pussy. Do you miss Simone or something?"

Vicious words left my lips with such venom that she looked at me in alarm. "Fuck that bitch."

Chance

"Simone is in Atlanta. She ran, Chance."

Figured that bitch would outsmart this shit. Her vindictive ass was always ahead of the game.

No matter how I reacted on the inside, my outer exterior remained cool and unalarmed as I sat across from the state's attorney. The attorneys that Gia hired were sitting next to me. They were posted like the Men in Black, all three of them.

Since my last visit with Gia, I decided to stop being a punk bitch. I needed to fight. I was guilty, but it wasn't all my fault. And now that they had Simone, it was a chess game; who was going to make the best move to ultimately win.

Simone would take no chances. She would take the deal and send me up the river for twenty-five to life.

"Ten years. We're offering you ten years, Chance."

I didn't know what to think when Thomas, one of my lawyers, spoke up. "In exchange of what?"

It sounded like he thought that I should actually consider this shit. That made vomit threaten to come up. At first, they were so sure about me being able to beat this shit. When they learned about the previous deal, they laughed at it and told me not to worry.

I wondered what evidence had come up that had convinced him otherwise.

"In exchange for his testimony against Simone."

"There is no evidence that my client, or Simone Campbell, were on that block the day of the murder," Alex, my other attorney, argued. "There is no evidence that my client is or knows Reginald Barner. There is no murder weapon. No DNA. Not even a fingerprint."

"He was with Simone the day of the murder."

"Circumstantial," Alex came back.

"He was arrested in the company of the woman that reported this murder." The state's attorney was practically laughing. "He grew up in the group home where the other suspect worked."

"Circumstantial."

Again, the state's attorney had a humored smirk on his face. "Well, people get convicted on circumstantial evidence all the time, now don't they?"

The state's attorney gathered his things without even announcing his exit. He stood and began to walk out. As he opened the door, he shot over his shoulder, "The deal is on the table, Chance. Think about it."

I looked at all three of my attorneys. I hoped that they had something soothing to tell me. I needed to be convinced that fighting this was the right thing to do.

I wanted to fight this. But if I could do ten years, rather than thirty, I was game. If they could get these charges dropped altogether, I was game for that shit too.

Unfortunately, confidence is the last thing that they gave me.

"He's right, Chance," Peter said, breaking my heart. "People get convicted on circumstantial evidence all the time, with even less evidence than what they have."

My heart dropped to my nut sack. "What the fuck? I thought y'all said I could beat this."

"We can. We can try," Alex said. "But ten years for a murder and attempted murder is a damn good deal. They want Simone. Not you, son. You'll have the chance of parole in eight years. It's nothing to sneeze at . . . Think about it."

Chapter Fourteen

Simone

It was a Tuesday morning. The sun was shining so bright that it made the ninety-degree July air feel like one hundred degrees. Every morning in the South was like a fresh start. And that morning was definitely a fresh start for me.

I was riding in a drop top Bentley that Teddy rented for our special day. Three days after asking me to marry him, I'd convinced him to allow us to marry in a quick courthouse ceremony. His parents were meeting us there. Jay wasn't invited.

I was wearing a white Dolce and Gabbana maxi dress. It was simple, but elegant enough to get married in at a courthouse. Teddy kept it street in jeans, but he wore a vest with a button up and slick Christian Louboutin loafers.

As we rode the highway towards downtown Atlanta, hand in hand, I really wished that this *was* real for me. I wished that this could have been me and Tre. I longed for the day that this could have been me and Omari. It saddened me that, after all the tricks, plots, and scheming, I wasn't marrying the man that I killed to get. I had played so many ratchet and deadly games of love and lust. Now I accidently ended up with a man that actually loved me unconditionally.

After we parked, Teddy hopped out of the car to open the door for me. His romantic gestures always pulled at my heartstrings. But they also pulled at my anger. It pissed me off that I could never get a nigga that I actually wanted to do these kinds of gentlemanly things for me. They always only wanted to fuck. They only wanted me to be a side bitch. They never thought I was good enough to commit to.

Teddy and I walked towards the courthouse hand in hand. So many people looked at us with adoring eyes. They could tell by his boyish smile, the romantic smile on my face, and my white dress that we were about to get married. Many men gave him an approving gesture, as we stood in line to fill out the paperwork. They thought him lucky to have me. Women looked at me curiously, wondering what I saw in him. Smirks replaced their curious grins as they figured that it must be the money that afforded him Christian Louboutin loafers and gold fronts more expensive than the cars they rode in.

His mom was waiting as we entered the room where the small quick ceremony was going to be held. Though I was playing a role, butterflies still consumed my being as we exchanged vows.

"I, Simone, take you, Theodore, to be my lawfully wedded husband, to have and to hold, from this day forward, for better, for worse, for richer, for poorer, in sickness and in health, until death do us part."

Death.

The word barely escaped me. For my heart to beat rhythmically, so much death consumed me. I had taken so many lives to make it to this place with one particular man. Dahlia was cold in the ground, lying next to her dead mother. But Omari wasn't standing in front of me.

"I, Theodore, take you, Simone, to be my lawfully wedded wife, to have and to hold, from this day forward, for better, for worse, for richer, for poorer, in sickness and in health, until death do us part."

He was indeed taking me for sickness, because I could not deny that I was a sick and twisted individual. Even as he slipped the eight-carat exquisite diamond ring on my finger, I tallied how much money I would get for it once I pawned it after I left this funny looking motherfucker.

Yet, pawning it was only additional financial security. Now that I was Mrs. Theodore Franklin, I had my very own bank account. Though it had only been funded with ten thousand dollars to start with, to ensure that I was comfortable marrying him, it was enough to get me on a plane to Mexico.

OMARI

That morning, Detective Howard called and asked me to come to the precinct that afternoon. I had a gut feeling that it wasn't good. But I had been running from this for long enough. There were so many rumors and speculations that it was time to face it all like the man that I should have been when Aeysha was alive.

Detective Howard actually looked shocked to see me when I entered the Homicide unit of the 9th District precinct. She quickly muttered something to the officer sitting across from her. I'd seen him the last time that I was there. They both quickly stood as I approached the desk.

"Mr. Sutton, come this way."

Like the last time that I was there, Detective Howard led me to the same hot office that we sat in before. Unlike last time, she was accompanied by the other officer. Unlike last time, it was something eerie about being there. They looked at me different.

"I called you down here because we need to have a serious discussion," she told me as I sat down at the desk. They both sat across from me. "This is Detective Ingram."

Detective Ingram didn't speak or smile a hello. He simply looked at me, sternly.

"Before we begin, we need to let you know that you don't have to share any information with us, and you have the right to an attorney."

All I could do was nod. Something told me that maybe I shouldn't talk to them. But my heart needed to know what they had to say.

There was a folder in her hand that she then put on the desk and opened. As she began to speak she reached into the folder.

"This is a picture of Chance Rogers and Simone Campbell at a gas station on October 30, 2013 at five forty-five in the afternoon."

She didn't have to explain to me what the date was and what the time meant, but she did, "An hour after Aeysha's murder."

As the blood began to rush from my head, she continued to lay it all on me. "This is a bank statement showing a withdrawal of twenty-five thousand dollars from Simone Campbell's bank account on December 10, 2013. This is a statement from her realtor indicating her previous refusal to sell her home and then suddenly requesting, rather urgently, I might add, that she sell her home on October 1, 2013."

Suddenly, my head was falling into the palm of my hand as my elbow rested on the table.

"Omari, honestly, a lot of this is circumstantial. But it's a fact that Simone and Chance knew each other. And it's a fact that Chance is a close friend of yours. The evidence points to Simone and Chance, and most likely you. You were cheating on Aeysha. You impregnated your neighbor and had a relationship with Simone Campbell during your relationship with Aeysha. Maybe you didn't want a family, the baby, or Aeysha…"

"What?!" I looked at that bitch like she was crazy. "So y'all the motherfuckas that planted this shit in Aeysha's family's head?! That I killed her?!"

She reacted to my anger like I was a psych patient off my meds. She was calm and still. She didn't even flinch. Her light brown eyes burned into mine as she held a smirk full of accusations.

"Son, if you had anything to do with this, the time is now to be honest." Now the other officer was attempting to pacify me with the bullshit. "The state's attorney takes honesty into account. If you work with us, we can try to get you a deal..."

I jumped up out of my seat so fast that he went for his pistol. Immediately, Detective Howard shot her hand out, signaling for him to stand down.

"Am I under arrest?"

"No," she answered calmly. "Not right now."

"Then I'm out."

Shit got blurry after that. I didn't even recall walking through the precinct towards the exit. It was like I was outside of my body watching my world cave in on me. All I remembered was the sudden feeling of wetness as the sun burned my eyes. It was raining heavily. But that didn't matter to me as I hopped in the Challenger and sped out of the precinct's parking lot. It was too much to take in. It was too much to realize. I was out of control with grief, guilt, and shock. It was all blinding me. I raced down 79th Street at sixty miles an hour. I switched lanes and ran lights. Everything was a blur. My mind was somewhere else. I couldn't think or see straight. All I could hear was a blaring horn and sirens coming towards me as I entered an intersection. I wondered if I'd blown a red light as I turned to look in its direction. The ambulance was coming towards me. We hit our brakes at the same time. The rain caused our tires to spin out of control. Visions of cars and trucks trying to avoid colliding with me were before me. The tree was coming towards me so fast. It was like it was racing towards me. The more I attempted to steer the car, the faster and further I flew towards the tree.

    And then...

GIA

I couldn't stand how Chance still looked so defeated. I wanted to slap some sense into him. It wasn't in his best interest to be so weak.

"Hey, baby," I greeted him as we barely hugged.

I hated that I couldn't hold him. It sickened me that I couldn't kiss his face. He hadn't even been locked up for that long and already he looked so different. The color was gone from his skin. His locs were wild and untamed.

"What's going on?"

I sat across from him as I insisted, "You tell me. How is your case going?"

There weren't many people in the visitation room today. I figured that the sudden instant downpour had stopped a lot of people from coming out. I was even soaked from head to toe, despite using an umbrella. My jeans heavily stuck to me. My wife beater looked like I was competing in a wet tee-shirt contest.

"I met with them a few days ago. It's not looking too good."

My head instantly began to pound. "What do you mean? I thought they said you had a chance?"

"They did, but I guess things have changed. The state's attorney met with me the other day. My lawyers were there. The state's attorney offered me a deal. Ten years. I could parole in eight."

"You took it?"

"No. But it's still on the table."

"What did your lawyers say you should do?"

"They said that all the evidence is still circumstantial, but people get convicted on circumstantial evidence every day."

I wanted to argue that, but I couldn't. Chance and I looked at each other. We both wore expressions of defeat. The lawyers were right. People got convicted on circumstantial evidence every day. Shit, innocent people were in jail rotting away for the rest of their lives.

"Well, take it then, Chance."

I didn't want him to be in jail, but eight years versus a lifetime was nothing. I could wait for him for eight years. I was willing to. I would visit him every week if he had to. Talk to him every day if I could– anything to make that time go by fast for both of us. After eight years he could live his life again.

But he groveled. Once again, surrender was over his face.

"You feel that guilty that you can't fight?"

Chance looked at me like I was crazy. "What you want me to do?"

"If they feel like you'll lose, take the deal, Chance. Tell on that bitch. Do what you gotta do. Why take the chance of spending the rest of your life in prison?"

"I spent most of my life in prison, so what the fuck does it matter?"

I was so heartbroken. I couldn't believe that he was giving up like this.

"And why do you give a fuck anyway?"

Chance harsh words threw me for a loop. "What do you mean?!"

"Why do you care? Why do you keep coming here? Why are you paying for my lawyers? This shit is over. I am in here for murder. Murder, Gia…"

"So what! I'm here because I care. I'm here because I love you. I know that you ain't use to that kinda shit, but that's what people do when they love somebody. They stick it out."

"Well, since you the motherfucka that put me in here, why don't you stop fighting for me?"

"Fuck you, Chance!"

I had to get the fuck up outta there before I caused a scene. I stood up and raced outta that motherfucker. His lame ass didn't even try to stop me. I couldn't believe that he was turning on me like this after all we'd been through. I been swinging from a pole with my pussy out for weeks just to get him a decent fucking lawyer, and he treats me like this!

Granted, he was right. I had started all of this shit with my temper tantrum. But I loved him so much that I'd spent every day since trying to fix it.

If he couldn't see that, fuck him.

Chapter Fifteen

Simone

Two days after Teddy and I got married, I figured it was time to bounce. He'd gone to take care of some business, so I had time to make my moves.

After showering and changing into a jogging suit, something comfortable for the long fight, I took the keys to the Range Rover and stuffed the suitcases that I stole from Teddy into the backseat. He'd bought me so many clothes and shoes that they filled three large suitcases. One thing that I wouldn't have to spend my money on once in Mexico was clothes. I was good on that for quite some time.

After that, I was headed to the nearby Chase. I had already called ahead and booked a flight with my debit card to Mexico City. I wasn't completely safe in Mexico. If the police found me, I knew that I could be extradited. But Mexico sounded like a far enough place where it would be harder for them to find me. I was buying myself enough time with Teddy's money to think of an even better plan.

Withdrawing the remaining nine thousand dollars from Teddy's account was as simple as filling out the deposit slip and waiting for the money counter to finish. Then, I was off to the airport. Just that easily, pounds of pressure were off my shoulders. There wasn't an ounce of me that felt bad for what I was doing. I had to look out for myself. I couldn't just sit in Atlanta waiting for the police to catch me. I couldn't continue to live my life in fear of using my ID at the wrong place. Even getting that account was a stretch.

Finally, I was approaching Hartsfield–Jackson Atlanta International Airport. I was sadder about leaving that Range Rover behind than I was about leaving Teddy. He had provided me with a life of luxury that I would probably never again be able to obtain. I wished that there was a better way. Even as I pulled into the parking lot, I brainstormed, attempting to come up with a plan that would allow me to stay in Atlanta and enjoy Teddy's money and security. But, just like over the past few weeks, I could come up with nothing that kept my freedom, except running.

I stored the keys in the glove compartment. I at least wanted Teddy to have the keys. I figured once Teddy reported the car stolen, if it sat in the parking lot long enough, it would be towed and he would be contacted.

I retrieved my bags from the back seat. A shuttle bus met me at the trunk. The driver took the bags, allowing me to take get comfortable on the shuttle. And that was it. I was off to Mexico City.

EBONI

"Hey, Fred. Is Omari here?"

I had been calling Omari for days with no answer. After calling him for the hundredth time and getting his voicemail, I'd driven by the spot to check up on him. Omari had been in a pretty fucked up mood the last couple of times that I saw him. He was constantly drinking and bitter. Not only was Aeysha's murder case getting to him, but I knew that, deep down inside, this beef between him and Capone was breaking his heart.

"Nah. You didn't hear?"

I stood there frozen, waiting for Fred to continue. I didn't like the sympathy in his eyes or the reluctance in his expression.

"He got in a pretty bad car accident."

My heart literally dropped. "What?! Is he okay?!"

"He's good. He broke his arm though, and he's banged up real bad."

I couldn't believe this! Omari was having the worst of luck. "Where is he?!"

"Christ Hospital."

I didn't even say goodbye before I turned and ran towards my truck. I could hear the kids whining, laughing, and playing as I approached the car. It drove me crazy even thinking of having to take their asses to a hospital, but I had no other choice.

"Mama, I thought we was goin' to see Omari." Lil' T was

looking at me like I was crazy as I started the car and peeled off.

"We are going to see Omari. He's not here though, baby. We have to go see him at the hospital. He got hurt in a car accident." Before I knew it, I was tearing up. I knew that Omari was essentially okay, but my heart broke for him. The obstacles that life was sending him through had to be unbearable. I worried about his health and his sanity. I couldn't fathom experiencing anymore death.

Over my thoughts, I could hear Lil' T asking me fifty million questions about Omari. Why was he in a car accident? Did he die? Who hit him? What was hurt on him? Yadda! Yadda! Yadda! I couldn't fucking think straight! I for damn sure couldn't take their asses to the hospital. I wouldn't be able to leave them in the waiting area and taking them into Omari's hospital room probably wouldn't be allowed. So I decided to drop them off at my mother's.

"Whoaaa!" Tasia and Lil' T yelled out in unison as I bent a corner so fast that I sent the kids flying to the right side of the car.

"Put your seat belts on!"

Luckily, my mama was sympathetic about Omari being in the hospital. When I got to her crib, she was on her way out to prayer service at church. She packed Tatiana, Lil' T, and Tasia in the car and took them with her.

I made it to Christ soon after that. I couldn't help but wonder what kind of condition Omari was in that he wasn't able to call me to tell me what happened. The possibilities scared the fuck out of me. Fred said that he was only banged up with a broken arm, so I prayed to God that that was accurate.

I could hear voices outside of Omari's hospital room as I approached the slightly ajar door. I recognized Omari's voice, so I let out a sigh of relief as I opened the door. I thanked God that he was at least coherent and speaking.

As I entered the room, holding Jamari, I noticed a much older woman sitting beside Omari. She favored him and looked familiar. I believed that it was his mother, who I'd seen at the apartment building a time or two when he lived there. Omari was sitting up in bed with bandages on his head, cuts and scrapes all over his face, and a very broken arm in a cast. He looked disheveled. He was unshaved. His locs, which were usually styled to perfection, were pulled back in a messy ponytail. His new growth was out of control.

However, he did look relieved to see me. "Hey, Eboni."

"Oh my God. What happened?!"

I raced towards him. As I stood next him, I softly touched his leg and he touched Jamari's face with his free arm.

"I got in a car accident. I accidently ran a light. It was raining, so I lost control and hit a tree."

"Why didn't you call me?!"

"My phone was shattered in the accident. I couldn't think of your number for shit. Paula went by your crib yesterday to tell you, but you weren't there."

Finally, after an hour, since I left the spot, I was able to relax. He was smiling and talkative, so I was appreciative that he seemed to be okay, except for his broken arm.

"Is anything else broken?"

"Nah. I'm fine. I had a concussion, so they are keeping me here for observation."

I couldn't help but notice how the older lady was looking at Jamari. She was gazing up at him. I thought I saw tears pooling in her eyes. Even Omari noticed how she was looking at my baby.

He chuckled at the other woman and said, "Yea, mama. That's my baby."

His mother let out a happy sigh of relief. She even squealed a little bit as she allowed her tears to fall.

She asked me, "Aren't you the girl that lived downstairs?"

Full of guilt, I simply nodded. She gave Omari and I judgmental motherly glares, but was too focused on Jamari to say the reprimanding words behind them. "Can I hold him?"

"Sure," I told her as I walked over to the other side of the room.

I handed Jamari to her and, as I did, he began to coo. She smiled adoringly at him. It was as if he was the best thing she'd laid her eyes on in a very long time.

She looked at me and said, "Thank you." Her voice was full of such joy, yet so much sorrow and regret. Her emotions were mixed, but I knew exactly what they meant. She and Omari had lost so much in such a short time. For the first time, I didn't feel a shred of embarrassment for having my baby. For the first time, I understood what "things happen for a reason" really meant.

SIMONE

"Group C is now allowed to board."

After sitting in the airport for an hour and sitting through a thirty-minute flight delay, I was finally boarding my flight. I slipped the iPad that I was using to browse the Internet into my Louis Vuitton Carry All bag and stood in line to board.

Glancing out of the window, I took a deep breath as I stared at the Delta plane. A plane had never looked so good to me in my life. As I browsed the Internet, I found a few hotels near the airport that were affordable. So I knew exactly where I was going once I arrived in Mexico City. There was a bit of anxiety in the back of my mind. I had no idea what I was going to do for money. Yet, anything was better than waiting in the United States like a sitting duck.

As I boarded the plane, pressure began to lift from my shoulders. I had spent the last year in pure anxiety: fear of losing Omari, the pressure of competing with a dead girl and her baby, and running from the law. Finally, it was all over. Life wasn't going to be perfect in Mexico, but it was going to be much more bearable.

Relief once again consumed me, as I got comfortable in my aisle seat. I was one of the last to board the plane, so I watched as the flight attendants prepared for takeoff. I went for my Beats headphones so that Anita Baker could sing me to sleep. After securing my seatbelt, I leaned back, closed my eyes, and relaxed for the first time in months.

However, the relaxation lasted all but seconds. I felt a tap on my shoulder. I figured that it was the flight attendant asking me to power off my music player during takeoff. Yet, when I opened my eyes, there wasn't a flight attendant standing over me. My heart threatened to cease beating as my eyes focused upon police officers surrounding my seat. I glanced at the front of the aircraft, and there were what looked like detectives standing there also.

Reluctantly, I pulled out my earphones.

"Simone Campbell, you're under arrest," the male officer nearest me barked.

"Who?" I tried to act like I didn't know who the fuck Simone was.

"Get up," he told me dismissively.

He moved further down the aisle and allowed the female officer to come closer. I remained seated like I didn't know what the fuck was going on. I cringed as the other passengers gawked at the scene. Some of them were even recording it with their phones.

"Ma'am, you're under arrest for the murder of Aeysha Walker." As she spoke, she reached down and unbuckled my seat belt. Then she grabbed me by the arm and snatched me out of my seat.

"Ow!"

She ignored me, bending my arm behind my back and cuffing me. "You have the right to remain silent. Anything you say or do can and will be used against you in the court of law. You have the right to an attorney. If you can't afford one, one will be appointed to you. Do you understand your rights?"

As they forced me down the aisle with my hands cuffed behind my back, it amazed me how this all felt like a dream. Just last year, I was living a normal life. Sure, I didn't have what and who I wanted, but I wasn't *this* – I wasn't a murderer. I hadn't killed anyone. I wasn't on the run. And I wasn't facing the end of my life.

"Do you understand your rights?"

I didn't understand what had happened to me. I didn't understand why I had become so desperate that I found myself here.

"Do you understand?!"

Tears came and began to flow. I was persistent when I was doing what I thought I had to do to get Omari. But now, as they led me off the plane, I knew that none of it was worth it. "Yes, I understand."

Chance

I was just chillin' in the television room staring at the news. I really wasn't paying it any attention. My mind was going at one hundred miles an hour.

I hadn't talked to Gia since she stormed out of her last visit. I called her every chance that I got, but she wouldn't answer.

I deserved that shit though. I was foul for how I talked to her. I lashed out at her when she didn't deserve it. Since the day that I met her, she'd done nothing but be there for me. When I was broke, she fucked with me. Even after knowing that I killed a woman, she stood by my side. Even while in jail, she was paying for my attorney. I was always too macho to admit that I didn't know how to accept love. I never had anyone who truly loved me and had my back. While growing up in Lexington, I thought that person was Simone. But Simone eventually showed her true colors. Time after time, I had turned my back on Gia, rejecting a love that I didn't know how to accept.

That was wrong. This was a time in my life when I needed somebody the most. Yet, I was pushing the one person away that didn't want anything else but to be behind me, having my back.

Just as I was considering calling Gia again before lockdown for the evening, Simone's face flashed across the television screen.

I nudged homeboy with the remote, who was sitting in front of me. "Yo', fam, turn that up."

I looked at the screen in horror. The anchor, Alicia Ramon, was standing in front of the Cook County building with a mic in one hand and an umbrella in the other. It was raining, and I envied the fact that she was out there, in freedom, able to feel the rain.

"We interrupt this program for news that is breaking right now. A suspected murderer was caught in Atlanta, Georgia at the Hartsfield–Jackson International Airport. Investigators say that this woman, Simone Campbell, is the suspect in a murder for hire. Right now, she is on her way to back to Chicago to Cook County jail where she will be arraigned on the charges of first-degree murder. The victim, Aeysha Walker, was killed in an apparent drive by shooting in October of last year. Investigators say that evidence since her death proved that in fact this was a murder for hire. Evidence shows that Simone Campbell paid twenty–five thousand dollars to the shooter..."

I couldn't listen to anymore. I stood, making a quick exit. I didn't know whether I should go lie down to stop my head from spinning. I headed for bathroom with an urge to purge the dry meatloaf and flavorless mashed potatoes that I had for dinner. But ever since I was a child, I hated throwing up. So I went back to my cell to fight the anxiety attack that was pummeling towards me like a fighting bull.

I fell into the bottom bunk. My body was so heavy with defeat. Now, the deal that was on the table sounded sweeter than candy. I knew that Simone was so dirty, so manipulative, and so evil, that she would pin this shit on me the first chance she got.

It was over for me.

SIMONE

I wasn't even questioned.

They didn't even ask me if I did it. They just hauled me off the plane. Two officers escorted me through the airport while the others followed. I was cuffed, so I couldn't hide my face from the camera flashes as I took the long walk through the airport. I held my head down, trying to allow my side bang to hide my face.

Outside of the airport were photographers and reporters. Prior to being arrested, I knew what I had done. But it didn't seem real. Nobody but Chance and I knew, so it didn't seem real. Even while at Teddy's home, I knew that I was being chased. But I thought that I could still flee and act like this shit never happened. But as I fought to hide from the light of the cameras and as I recognized anchors that previously told me of different crimes in Atlanta as I watched the news every morning and evening, I had the horrifying realization that shit had just gotten all the way real.

I had to think of something. As they threw me in the back of the squad car that was waiting outside of the airport, I began to dissect what possible evidence they had against me.

"Where are you taking me?"

The female officer laughed at me like I had told a joke. "You're going back to Chicago. On the first thing smoking."

"When can I speak to a lawyer?"

"As soon as you get back to Chicago."

In their eyes, I was guilty. I knew that nobody was going to help me. It was best that I shut the fuck up until I got back to Chicago and spoke to an attorney.

Chapter Sixteen

Omari

"We got her, Omari."

I looked at Detective Howard like she was out of her fucking mind.

"No shit," I told her.

Eboni looked at me like I was crazy for talking to Detective Howard that way. Even her partner, Detective Ingram, gave me a warning glare. I didn't give a fuck though. This bitch was standing here trying to play me. No shit Simone got arrested. It had been all over the evening and morning news.

It was one thing to accuse me of murdering Aeysha, but it was another to accuse me of murdering her on top of treating me like a dumbass.

"Can I help y'all?"

I didn't even know why these motherfuckers were in my hospital room. They were the reason why I was in the hospital in the first place. This case and their accusations had me so gone in the head that I damn near killed myself.

"You know that once we have her in our custody, she is going to sing like bird."

I didn't even have a response for Detective Howard. The police were real good at pinning shit on the innocent. I wasn't about to give them nothing to help put me away by saying anything stupid. If they wanted to try pinning this bogus charge on me, they could do it by themselves. I wasn't saying shit.

But they were persistent on making me give them information that I didn't have. Detective Howard bent down and brought her face close to my ear. She was so close that I could smell the spearmint gum that she was chewing.

"Are you sure that you don't have anything to tell us, Omari? Now is the time."

I actually wished that I knew what the fuck was going on. As I watched the news coverage over and over again, I tried to piece together the puzzle. This shit was so outlandish that it was unbelievable. The evidence against Chance and Simone made sense. But that could be said about the evidence that they were trying to pin on me.

And I *knew* that I was innocent.

I turned to make eye contact with Detective Howard. I could see Eboni out of my peripheral holding Jamari close to her chest. She looked like a deer caught in headlights. I felt that way on the inside, but I wasn't about to let anybody see it.

I stared Detective Howard down. We were so close that we exchanged breath. "Unless I'm being placed under arrest, you can leave, or stand there looking at me, because I don't have shit to say."

Her partner flexed like he had an issue with my attitude. Luckily, I was in a hospital bed with a bad arm, so they couldn't do much to me without being criminally negligent.

With a smirk, Detective Howard told me, "Have a good a day, Mr. Sutton."

I watched her as they left with a grimace hovering in my throat. I had never been so sick of seeing a broad in my life.

As soon as the door closed, Eboni went in. "What the fuck are they talking about, Omari?"

I played dumb. "Huh?"

"What are they expecting you to tell them?"

"Hell if I know, Eboni!"

When she actually gave me a questioning look, my heart broke. "What? You think I had something to do with it too?"

"No, but…"

"But nothing then! Fuck!"

My anger wasn't towards her. I had so much anger going in so many different directions that I couldn't even think or see straight. I did know that Eboni was the most innocent of them all. And I knew for damn sure that one of those directions was coming directly at me.

I tried to calm down. I tried to look at her and allow my eyes to tell her what my mouth was too tired to explain. But no matter how much Eboni tried, I still saw that residue of doubt on the top of her perspiring brown skin.

SIMONE

During the entire eight-hour drive to Chicago, I thought about running.

I thought about waiting until they allowed the three prisoners on board to use the bathroom, fighting my way out, and running into the woods along the highway rest areas.

My night in the holding cell was like a living nightmare. Crack heads and prostitutes surrounded me in every cell. They talked and rambled all night, like being locked up was nothing but a walk in the park to them. They bragged about the crimes they committed. One even talked freely about having Hepatitis C and HIV as she hacked and damn near coughed up a lung all fucking night.

I couldn't imagine spending the rest of my days with those whores and drug-addicted bitches. I didn't belong in prison with those kinds of people. That wasn't me. I didn't belong on a stankin' ass bus in an itchy ass jumpsuit with my wrist cuffed to a bench. I was educated. I was beautiful. I had money. As I sat on that bus, staring at the freedom in the eyes of the people that rode by, I wondered how in the fuck I got so desperate that I found myself on a bus as a murderer. I wondered where I hit that point of no return and never looked back. I wondered what drove me to smother a helpless baby. I wondered which heartbreak it was that brought me to the point that I refused to lose so much that I was willing to *take* my win. I wondered, after them niggas fucked and got sucked and went back to those undeserving bitches, what they were doing while I was on a bus about to face twenty-five to life.

Suddenly, it didn't seem worth it. When I thought that having Omari was everything, even more than breathing, every trick, every lie, and every bullet was no longer worth it.

Despite that knowledge, I refused to be defeated. I planned to live my life apologetic and with a lesson learned, *but free*. As I sat in the cell last night, I was in the company of a woman that was married to a man that had been convicted of murdering his business partner. She helped me realize that the evidence that they could have was very little. As long as they didn't have a witness or a gun with my prints, I had a fighting chance.

Therefore, once we arrived on 26th and California at the Cook County jail, and I was hauled into a small grey room, I decided to say nothing and just take my chances.

I recognized Detective Howard as she walked into the room followed by a white man, who appeared to be a detective as well. They both appeared to be terribly hot. In slacks and long sleeved button ups, they were both sweating like the pigs that they were.

As I got off of the bus, it felt like Georgia heat. It had to be eighty some odd degrees in the early evening on the July day. Even in the room, I sweat under the jumpsuit that I was regretfully sporting.

"Well, hello there, Ms. Campbell."

I didn't utter, smirk, or speak. I just sat with one arm cuffed to a rail and my other holding up my very heavy and tired head.

"You remember me, I'm sure. This is my partner, Detective Ingram."

I looked at her, my eyes telling her to get on with it.

"We have a lot of evidence against you and Chance Rogers."

And that is when the acting began. "Chance? My client? What does he have to do with this?"

Smirking, she pulled out a picture from the manila folder that she was holding. She laid a picture of Chance and I before me. I recognized what we were wearing and knew that it was the day that he killed Aeysha.

"Okay," I replied, looking at the picture. "That's me and Chance. What is your point?"

"That is the day that Aeysha Walker was murdered. You do know who Aeysha was, right? Omari's pregnant girlfriend. The woman he didn't want to leave even though he was sleeping with you."

Even though it was in the past, it still cut like a knife to hear such true words. I fought hard to keep my composure.

"Me and Omari are no longer in a relationship. And I looked out for Chance on many occasions while he lived in Lexington and after he moved into transitional housing. I was more than his mentor. We were friends. He was down on his luck. That day, I was giving him a few dollars to help him get by. If you scan the surveillance of many other stores and gas stations in the area, you will see us together."

"Aren't these text messages between you and Chance discussing Aeysha's murder?"

I quickly glanced at the papers that she sat before me. I hid the gut wrenching reaction that I felt. I wondered how in the hell they got those text message transcripts. But I continued to act to save my life.

I laughed while saying. "What is this? Are you trying to pin this murder on me? This isn't even Chance's phone number. And I didn't read one sentence in these transcripts of me admitting to anything. I want a lawyer..."

"Ms. Campbell..."

"I do not want to talk to you any further. I want a lawyer."

They had no choice but to end their interrogation. For once since being arrested, I had some sense of relief. If this was all the evidence that they had, I had a chance. They had no concrete evidence or no smoking gun.

I still had a chance.

Chapter Seventeen

Omari

"Omari!"

Paula jumped up from the kitchen table. She was so happy to see me. She acted like I was previously on my deathbed or something. She even threw her arms around me and hugged me tight, careful not to touch my broken arm.

"Oh my goodness! Look at your face!" She touched my face, examining the many cuts and scrapes, some that had been closed with a few stitches.

"I'm okay, Paula. Is anybody here?"

"Fred left to go get us some breakfast."

"Oh yea? I'm pretty hungry myself. Let me call him and tell him to grab me something."

I sat down at the table and took my cell from my pocket. Paula sat across from me and continued to weigh the work that she was bagging. I was glad that business was still running smoothly, even though I spent a few days away in the hospital. I was released that morning and couldn't have been happier. I was going crazy being locked up in there.

Fred was just as excited to hear that I was out of the hospital as Paula was to see me. It felt good to know that my absence even mattered to them. I realized that, even though I lost one family, I had truly gained another that loved me and that I had to stay strong enough to take care of.

As I hung up the call with Fred, Paula sat back with a long sigh and looked at me hesitantly.

Reluctantly, I asked her, "What's wrong?"

I didn't want to hear any bullshit, nor could I really handle any bad news. But, since I was the boss, they always felt like they had to tell me every little thing.

"I gotta tell you something, boss."

"What's up?"

"Well, I been hearing Fred and Capone talk about everything that's going on with Aeysha's case and all this shit with Chance and Simone being accused of having something to do with it." She rocked, scratched, and pulled her dirty blond hair nervously as she hesitantly continued. "You know I don't really get into your business. I just come here and do my job, because, even though I love you to death, I need this money and the warm place to crash when I'm working."

I looked at her curiously, wondering what the fuck she was rambling about. "Okay. And?"

"Well, a few months ago, right before Simone got hurt, she came here to talk to me. She wanted me to help her do something."

I sat up, giving her my full attention. "Help her do what?"

She took another deep breath. She actually looked scared. I had never seen Paula so timid before. She was usually fearless, willing to do whatever. "She asked me to help her steal a baby... your sister's baby."

That shit hit me so hard that it took my breath away. I could barely get the words out as I asked, "She what?"

I'd heard her, but I couldn't fucking believe my ears.

"Your sister was scheduled for a c-section, right? Simone told me that she needed to steal a baby because she didn't know how to tell you that she wasn't really knocked up. Simone told me the whole plan. She said that she would tell you that she was going out of town for work somewhere too far for you to get to in time when she called claiming to go into labor. Instead, we were going to be in Indianapolis, waiting on Erica to leave the hospital with her baby. Then I was supposed to carjack her and take her baby."

The shit sounded absolutely ridiculous, especially coming from a dope fiend. But Paula was never one to lie to me. No matter her financial situation or being on dope, she'd never as much as stolen from me.

As if she was further trying to convince me, she told me, "She said that since you and your sister never saw each other that she should be able to pull it off. But I don't know what the fuck that bitch was smoking, because obviously she couldn't have pulled no shit off like that without somebody finding out. I wanted to say something, but she threatened to tell you that I stole those bricks if I didn't help her. I didn't want to lose my job. Fred told me that she supposedly told you that she got an abortion. That's not true though, boss. She was never pregnant. And I'm glad she ended up getting her ass whooped, because that chick was about to do something real crazy to get you a baby if she hadn't been stopped."

I jumped out of my seat. The chair made such a loud noise as it hit the wall that Paula jumped. She cringed, thinking that I was about to hit her, and relaxed once I walked by her and towards the door.

"Where you goin', boss?!" She was calling after me as I left out. I could hear her in the doorway as I ran down the steps. "Boss!"

"Don't be here when I get back, Paula! Close up! Tell Fred to go home!"

SIMONE

The next morning was my bail hearing. So I sat on a bench behind the courtroom, along with other female prisoners, for hours waiting for my case to come up.

Once I was finally allowed a phone call last night, I called Teddy. I figured that I could give him some excuse about why I was gone and why I had been arrested. I hoped that he was gullible enough to send me a good attorney and pay my bail, if it was granted. He never answered the phone, so I sobbed uncontrollably into his voicemail while giving him a heartfelt spiel about getting cold feet with the marriage, flying to Mexico to clear my head, and being surprisingly arrested for some shit linked to my crazy ex back in Chicago.

It was a farfetched story, but as my name was called by a white older gentleman in a suit holding a rather thick folder, I guess it worked.

"Ms. Simone Campbell?" He looked over the bench of prisoners curiously.

I waved my only free hand to get his attention, since my other was cuffed to a bar on the bench. "I'm Simone Campbell."

I wondered who he was. Since I hadn't heard from Teddy, I requested a public defender. Yet, this was not a public defender. He was a high-powered attorney definitely. His suit was Armani. His shoes were Gucci. His watch was Rolex.

"Hi, Simone. Your spouse sent me," he told me quietly as he sat beside me.

I let out a huge sigh of relief; thankful that Teddy's naïveté was still in my favor.

Because I was under arrest, he couldn't take me to a private room to talk to me. We had to speak in front of the other prisoners who broke their necks to hear our conversation. Some of their bum asses even talked over him, asking if he could represent them.

He ignored them and gave me his fullest attention. "I'm going to try my best to get you bail."

"Do I have a good chance?"

He smirked and rolled his eyes as if that answer was obvious. "Of course. This evidence is weak," he told me as he waved the folder effortlessly in the air as if its contents meant nothing.

I let out another huge sigh of relief. If he felt like I could get bail, then I had a chance to get the fuck up out of here and back on a plane.

"There is no connection to you and this crime. They don't have concrete evidence. At the least, you should be able to fight this out on bail."

Perfect! I couldn't have been happier. Little did he know, I wasn't going fight a gawd damn thing. Once I was granted bail, I was going to get the fuck outta dodge.

And that is exactly what happened. Once I was before the judge, my attorney argued my case like a pro. Hell, he had *me* convinced that I was innocent.

"Your Honor, even if you look at those text message transcripts, my client never mentions or refers to a murder. This is all circumstantial evidence. My client does not have a criminal record. She does not have as much as a parking ticket..."

"She is flight risk," the state's attorney spewed. "She was caught on a flight to Mexico..."

"On a vacation. She'd just gotten married," he lied eloquently. "Look, if the State fears that my client is a flight risk, then put her on house arrest. She agrees to that."

Submissively, I nodded in agreement as the judge eyed me suspiciously.

With a heavy sigh, the judge finally made a decision. "Defendant is granted bail."

I was so relieved that the stresses left my body with a loud sigh of relief.

The state's attorney was livid. "Your Honor!"

But the judged ignored him. "The defendant is to wear electronic monitoring and does not have permission to leave so much as Cook County. The moment you fail to adhere to the guidelines of bail, you will be locked up, Ms. Campbell. Do you understand?"

Quickly, I told her, "Yes, ma'am."

Then the next case was called, and I was hauled off to the back for processing. My attorney stayed there right beside me, going over the case and the evidence against me. I didn't give a shit though. I barely listened. I was too busy figuring out how the fuck to get on a bus to the airport once I was released and given my possessions.

The attorney noticed me looking around as we stepped outside into the lobby of Cook County. I was trying to figure out where the nearest exit was.

He then told me, "Your spouse is waiting for you."

Immediately, I was thrown off. I couldn't believe that Teddy had managed to get to Chicago so fast. But considering his length of coins, it was totally possible for him to have hired me an attorney and gotten to Chicago in a matter of hours.

As the attorney walked me towards the waiting area where I suspected Teddy was, I figured that I would even be able to talk Teddy into taking me back to Atlanta. I could at least save my money and use his to get me half way across the country.

I could ditch his ass from there.

But, to my utter shock and amazement, it was not Teddy waiting in the lobby to greet me.

It was Omari.

"Mr. Sutton, I hope you're satisfied with today's proceedings."

When Omari smiled, no matter the situation, I fell in love all over again.

"I sure am," he told my attorney. "I knew you could do it. Ching told me that you were a beast in the courtroom. I appreciate you looking out for my lady. When can we meet with you to talk about her case?"

"Monday morning, for sure. Just give me a call."

As we said our goodbyes, my heart was pounding. I didn't know what to say. I didn't know what Omari knew. Obviously, he didn't know or believe anything since he'd hired my defense.

Confusion slowly began to leave me as he grabbed my hand lovingly and led me towards the exit. We walked in silence as we fought the crowds of people that were going in and out of the County building.

His Challenger was parked right outside. He opened the door for me and, for a split second, I thought about running. I couldn't go back with him. Whether he knew the truth or not, I had to bounce. But for the sake of buying time, I allowed him to assist me into the passenger seat.

Once he climbed in, I attempted to explain everything. "Omari, I have no idea what's going on. It's ridiculous that they would even think that I would have anything to do with Aeysha's death."

After quickly turning the ignition, he held my hand, intertwining our fingers while saying, "I know, babe. This shit is crazy. They even accused me of the shit. They just fishin'. We gon' get you out of this shit though." Then he kissed the back of my hand.

No matter the pure hell that I was in, his full dark lips felt good against my skin.

"Where have you been?"

It didn't even seem like Omari was mad at me. He'd always had a very cool demeanor. That's why I was able to get so much shit past him. But he actually looked relieved to see me.

"I went to Atlanta to get away and clear my head. Our relationship was so rocky after I got that abortion. You were hurt. I was hurt. I just wanted to get away."

"So, you just sold your condo, quit your job, and left?"

I hadn't sold the condo. But I sighed as I replied, "I know it was extreme, but I didn't know what else to do, Omari. I had been living in another woman's shadow for a year. I was tired of it. I needed to start fresh."

As he approached the red light and brought the car to a stop, he looked me in my eyes. Those gray eyes sent all kinds of submission and admiration through me. Once back in his presence, I was once again a fool in love, lust, and obsession.

"Without me?" I had never heard so much sadness in his voice.

"It was a stupid decision. I'm sorry."

Again, he kissed the back of my hand. Then he asked, "Are you hungry? I know that County food sucks."

I laughed as my heart continued to fill with relief. "I'm starving."

"Good. Me too. Let's go eat."

Omari

After we grabbed a bite to eat, I took Simone back to the spot. Thankfully, Paula had closed up shop like I told her to. There wasn't a dope boy in sight. But unfortunately, Eboni was pulling up just as Simone and I were getting out of the car.

I fought hard not to catch her eye. She fought harder to catch mine as she straight jumped out of her truck. "Omari!"

I silently sighed with frustration. Simone glanced at Eboni. When she recognized who Eboni was, she rolled her eyes hard as hell. Then she had the nerve to look at me like I was crazy.

This bitch had balls bigger than me.

"What the fuck is going on?!" Eboni wasn't even trying to hide her anger. She was pissed about Simone being there.

She actually approached me and Simone as we walked towards the house like she was ready to scrap.

Simone flipped her hair, turned her nose up at Eboni, and kept walking towards the house. I stood in Eboni's path, blocking her from walking any further.

"Why the fuck is she here, Omari?!"

Before I could say anything, Simone snapped back as she stood on the porch. "Because he wants me to be obviously! Why the fuck are you here?!"

Eboni tried to go through me like a linebacker. I aggressively grabbed her by the shoulders. My strength surprised her. She looked at me like I was crazy.

"Go home, Eboni," I told her.

She looked at me in shock and full of hurt. "Go home? Are you fucking serious?"

Behind me, Simone shouted, "He sound serious, don't he?!"

But this time Eboni ignored her. She stood looking me in the eye like I had lost my mind. "That pussy that good, huh?"

Nonchalantly, I stuffed my hands in the pockets of my jeans and shrugged. "Go home, Eboni."

She flipped me off before turning and stomping away. As I turned around, Simone had a smug smile on her face. I followed her into the crib, taking her purse and bags from her to help her along the way.

"God, this place stinks," she fussed as we walked through the kitchen.

"It's a trap. What you expect?"

"For it to be as clean as I left it. Ew!"

She continued to walk through the house like she owned the motherfucker. I followed her while discreetly digging my hand through her purse. I found what I was looking for as we entered the living room. She was too busy talking to even pay attention to the fact that I had her phone.

I just had to see for myself.

While I was in the hospital, I'd logged onto Facebook to look at Aeysha's Facebook page. I had to do a lot of scrolling past messages from her friends and family posted on her wall to find her status messages from when she was alive. I found the messages announcing her pregnancy. I can't even explain the feeling I got when I realized that the date correlated with the date that Simone decided to sell her crib. I had the same phone for years. So I was even able to scroll through my text messages back to last year, to the day of Aeysha's murder. Simone was texting me as usual. Even while I was at the store while Aeysha was being gunned down. Simone told me that she was stuck at work doing overtime, not at a gas station with Chance.

"What are you doing?!"

She'd finally stopped talking long enough to realize that the phone in my hand was hers. She tried to snatch it from me, but I was too tall for her to reach it.

"Give me my phone, Omari!"

I swatted her away as she reached for the phone. I backed away and turned my back. "Why you still got this phone? Thought it was cut off?"

"My music is still on there! Give it to me!"

I only had to punch in the area code and first three digits of Aeysha's old cell number before the contact saved as "HER" popped up.

I lost it.

I completely fucking lost it.

I never thought that I could beat a woman like that. I turned around and punched Simone so hard that she flew back onto the couch.

I beat Simone's ass like she was a nigga on the street.

"Bitch, you still got her fucking number in your phone!"

My fist made brutal contact with her face over and over again. I could feel her feminine scratches as she attempted to claw her way out from under me as I pummeled her on the sofa.

I could also feel her blood as it flew from her mouth and nose and onto my face and wife beater.

I punched her until her blood blurred my vision. I tried to knock the living shit out of her until I was tired and out of breath.

Once I felt her body relax, something in me just stopped. I jumped up, snatched the nine from waist and pointed it at her. But as I glared at her bleeding and moaning in agony, laying damn near lifeless across the sofa, a realization heavier than any guilt came over me.

I'd done this. Even if Simone set the shit up, I did this. Me and my dick. Me and my stupid decisions. Me and my greed for pussy. That's what got killed Aeysha.

Not Simone.

Not Chance.

Me.

Before I knew it, I'd turned the gun on myself. I stood in the living room breathing uncontrollably with the gun to my temple.

"Fam, what the fuck?!"

The voice all but scared the shit out of me. I spun around and pointed the gun at Capone. It was a reflex. We both knew that. I lowered my stance when I realized that it was him. As he rushed towards me, I broke down into guilty tears.

"Bro, what is you doin'?"

I could hear Capone as he hovered over my body. I had dropped to my knees and was gripping the gun, ready to aim it at myself and shoot.

This was all my fault. I'd killed Aeysha. No matter how much I wanted to punish Simone and Chance, the people who'd pulled the trigger, I was the one that ultimately set it up with my inability to love Aeysha as faithfully as I should.

"Bro, please. C'mon, man. Don't do this. It's not worth it. What about your mother? What about Jamari? What about me? You got a lot to live for, my nigga. You gotta get it together."

I didn't fight Capone as eased the gun out of my hand. I was still bawling uncontrollably. It was crazy how, along with the guilt, there was some relief. No matter how much I didn't like the taste of them, I had answers.

I also didn't fight when I saw Simone slip by me and Capone as he continued to console me in the middle of the floor. Through tears, I watched her stumble down the hall while holding her face.

"Let her leave," Capone told me. "She ain't worth it, bro. She ain't worth losing your life or freedom for. We need you. Just let her go."

SIMONE

My vision was blurry as I walked down the street. Children and young thugs looked at me like I was crazy. I tried to hide my face with my hair, but the afternoon sun was still shining brightly against it.

Three young girls playing jump rope in the middle of a side street off of 147th looked at me with bulging eyes as I walked by them.

One of them was even squealing, "Daaaaamn!"

My head was pounding. My eyes were beginning to swell shut. My nose was obviously very broken. The fat on the inside of my lip was spewing out of an open laceration.

I was sure that I looked like walking death.

I'd left out of the house so fast that I left my purse. But I wasn't desperate enough to go back for the cash that I needed. I felt my pockets, relieved that I felt a card. I hoped that it was a credit or debit card, but it was only my ID. I could not go back to Omari's house for my purse. If necessary, I would sleep on the street before I went back and asked for death, because Omari was surely in the mindset to kill me with his bare hands.

He knew. He knew that I had killed Aeysha, and, unless I got the fuck out of town, he would either kill me or tell the police. Either way I was fucked.

I had no choice but to do whatever necessary to run as far

away as I could. But without a dime, without even a cell phone, I was fucking screwed.

Besides a face that looked like I had lost a fight to Mayweather, I was okay. I figured that maybe I could hitchhike my way to a women's shelter, blame my face on that same abusive ex that was in my imagination, and at least have a place to sleep for a few days until I figured out how to get out of town. The sheriff was supposed to come to my condo the following day to apply my house arrest bracelet. After not getting an answer, I knew that there would be a warrant out for my arrest. So, I didn't have much time to get the fuck out of town.

The little girls behind me caught my attention. I had nearly reached the corner when I heard them squealing again.

Only this time, they weren't teasing me.

They were warning me.

"Watch out!"

"Oh my God!"

"Run, lady!"

Just as I turned around to see what they were talking about, my face was met with such force that it sent me flying backwards towards the city concrete.

Just as I began to sink into unconsciousness, I could hear the little girls screaming, their voices becoming further and further in the distance as if they were running away.

Then, I was out cold.

EBONI

"Lil' T, sit the fuck down! NOW!"

All the kids jumped at the sudden rage in my voice. Even Jamari jumped in his own skin as I held him and rocked with anger back and forth on the couch.

"Ooo, mama, you cussed." Tasia was standing in front of me with her thumb in her mouth, with the nerve to chastise me with her little toddler ass.

"Go in your rooms!"

"Mama, it's hot in our rooms," Lil' T pouted.

"Go in your rooms now! And do NOT come out unless I say so."

I was furious! I didn't even hear their little asses as they cried and complained while reluctantly walking to the back of the house. I was so pissed off. I couldn't believe Omari! I couldn't believe that he was so fucking stupid and naive for this bitch!

I was really starting to think that just maybe he did have something to do with Aeysha getting killed. There wasn't any other way that Omari could be gullible enough to turn the other cheek knowing how much evidence they had against this bitch.

He had been so tight lipped about what the fuck was going down, but the shit was all over the news. Chance had grown up in the housing where Simone worked. Supposedly there was evidence of this bitch paying him twenty-five thousand dollars. The fact that the detectives questioned this nigga at the hospital and he didn't say shit against this bitch was blowing me. I didn't give a fuck how good she fucked and sucked him, even if the evidence against her wasn't a hundred percent concrete, *I* had told him myself how shady that bitch was. He'd seen the shit in his own phone! If the bitch was conniving enough to pull some desperate slick moves like what I'd seen, there was no question what she was capable of.

The fact that, after all of this, this nigga had the audacity to obviously bail this bitch out of jail was just confirmation that they both had Chance kill Aeysha.

The doorbell rang, snatching me out of my enraged trance. I was so lost in my own thoughts that I hadn't even noticed that Jamari had fallen asleep. I placed him in the bassinet next to the couch. Then I reluctantly shuffled over to the front door to see who the fuck it was. It was probably them bad ass fucking kids from upstairs. And I was in a great mood to tell they motherfucking asses off. They could even tell they mama exactly what the fuck I said after I cussed them out so that I could give that bitch a piece of my mind too.

I was ready to unleash on a motherfucker in the worse way.

I snatched the front door open, expecting to see them bad ass snot nosed kids. But an even worse sight was standing before me. Omari couldn't even look at me. He had a face full of tears and a shirt full of blood. He looked so torn as tears rolled down his face. He was looking around the hallway and at and up the stairs.

I knew what he was thinking. I knew that the sight of the stairs reminded him of Aeysha. I knew that the smell of the building put him in the mind of her.

I took his hand and quickly ushered him inside of my apartment. I practically dragged him through the apartment towards my bedroom. I closed the door to keep the kids from coming in. The baby monitor would let me know if Jamari woke up.

I sat Omari on the bed and sat close to him. I wanted to ask him what the fuck had happened. With so much blood all over him, I wondered what he'd done to Simone.

Before I could say or ask anything, he began to wail loudly. I wrapped my arms around him. With arms very petite in comparison to his mass, I could barely hold him as he rocked back and forth, stomped and wept with a deep moan into my chest.

When he collapsed backward on the bed, I collapsed with him. I held him with all of my might as he literally screamed into my chest. There was so much hurt in his cries. I began to cry as well because I knew that his tears weren't just for Aeysha and Dahlia. They were for him, for his guilt. Outside of my anger, I knew better than to believe that he would ever set up Aeysha's murder.

But he knew. He knew that his bad choices and his dick had indirectly pulled the trigger.

Chapter Eighteen

Chance

"I want to just take the deal."

I thought that they would relax when they heard that. But Peter, Alex, and, my third attorney, Thomas, just looked at me from across the table in the visitation room of the Cook County Jail.

Before my preliminary hearing, they wanted to talk over the case, evidence, and strategy on getting the case dropped.

I didn't think known of that was necessary. Now that Simone had been charged, I knew that she would turn on me in any minute. I would rather confess and take the ten years than wait for her to send me up the river and face twenty-five to life for killing a pregnant woman.

"Honestly, Chance, I think you should allow us to fight this out today," Thomas told me.

"What if they take the deal off the table now that they have Simone?"

"They have Simone, but she isn't talking. For now, they still need you," Alex explained. "Lets see how today goes. If we lose the battle, then we will talk deal."

For twenty minutes, they explained to me how all of the

evidence was circumstantial against me. There was no weapon or witnesses. There was no proof that I was this Reginald Barner who had been in communication with Simone. There was no evidence of me making big purchases after allegedly receiving this payment from Simone for killing Aeysha. Gia being a stripper was a plus. She could have easily been dating Reginald Barner and me at the same time. They even had a signed statement from her denying that I was Reginald Barner. And Simone herself had even confessed during her questioning that I was simply one of her clients who she helped out from time to time once I'd moved into transitional housing.

They told me that for some judges this would be enough to allow the case to proceed. However, if I had a sympathetic and rational judge, I might be allowed to go free with the opportunity to recharge me once the police obtained more sufficient evidence.

I heard them, but it was all going over my head. I sat across from them, staring blankly, as October 30, 2013 played over and over again in my mind like a bad movie. I tried to figure out where I had gotten so desperate that I would point that gun at such a beautiful girl. I wondered how hungry I was to survive to pull that trigger after seeing her horrified face. I wondered how evil Simone could really be that she could smile with such satisfaction while watching Aeysha's body fall.

I even gave the movie alternate endings. I wondered how my life would be now had I told Simone no. I wondered how many lives would have been saved had I told the police of her plan.

I wondered how much better it would have felt facing a murder charge if I had have turned the gun on Simone, rather than that innocent Aeysha.

SIMONE

I woke up tied to a bedpost by every limb. I was bound at the wrists and ankles so tight that every movement hurt. Through grogginess, the events from the night before began to slowly come back to me.

I came to in the trunk of a car. It was dark and loud. Music was coming through the speaker next to me. I tried to move, but my ankles and wrist were bound. Even as I thought back to it, I began to tear up as I remembered the car slowing down, parking, and then the trunk opening a few minutes later.

At first, I couldn't see who opened the trunk. The sun was shining so bright that it was blinding me. But as he bent down to get me out of the trunk, Jimmy's face was revealed to me. Despite being bound by the ankles and wrists, I tried to kick and punch. Despite my mouth being bound by duct tape, I screamed as loud as I could.

We were in the back of a two flat. There was no backyard. We were in a parking lot. Behind us was a hill. On top of the hill were train tracks. Just as he began to carry me towards the door, a Metra train began to rumble by.

It was hard for him to unlock the door with me in his arms. But he managed to do so, despite me squirming to get free. Once inside the hallway, he dropped me on the floor and dragged me by a washer and dryer. The skin on my back burned against the rug. He hurriedly opened another door and practically threw me into the apartment. It smelled like cigarette smoke. The only thing in the living room was a sofa and a television that sat on the floor. It was worse than any trap house that Omari owned. Even the bed that he flung me on inside the bedroom was a pissy stank mattress and a bed rail.

"This time, I am going to make sure I kill you," was what he said to me as he began to tie me to the bed. "But first we're going to have some fun."

Every time I attempted to fight, he violently hit me in any organ closest to him. I regurgitated when he would pound me in my stomach. I was forced to swallow my vomit before I choked on it because the duct tape was holding my mouth closed.

With a pair of scissors, he cut my clothes from my body. I lay shivering as he removed my top, bra, and jogging suit. He actually showed signs of lust at the sight of my nakedness, and I cringed. I could do nothing as he lay on top of me. It burned as he penetrated me. I was dry as the Sahara. The friction was threatening to start a fire.

He raped me all night. He would ejaculate and leave the room with no words. I knew that he was intent on killing me, since he so easily deposited his semen inside of me. Then he would return after an hour or two with his hard dick protruding from his cargo pants. And all I could do was cry. I would cry myself to sleep and wake up to him forcefully penetrating me. As the night wore on, my vagina and its walls began to swell. He would force his way past the swelling with such force that it felt like he was ripping me open.

When he was tired of my vagina, he pushed his way into my ass. I screamed at a high pitch, but it was muffled by the duct tape. I began to feel wetness. But I knew that it wasn't my juices. I was sure that it was blood.

    I still lay there naked and shivering wondering when he would return. It scared the shit out of me to think what he would do when he returned. The air conditioner was on, fighting the stubborn ninety-degree summer air. Yet, I was so cold that the goose bumps on my skin were creating mountains. My tears dried and froze every time they fell from my eyes. I could hear him outside of the closed door. The television was on. I could smell cigarette smoke. I could hear movement about the apartment. But he never said a word.

    That is, until the door finally slowly creaked open. There he stood. I kept thinking that this is the same man that I, along with Tammy, hung out with countless times. This was the same man that begged me to tell him where she was hiding, and I told him, out of jealousy. He knew that I killed the love of his life. And he was pissed that I'd taken her from him. When I saw the knife in his hand, I pissed myself. Yet, it was so cold, that the warmth of the urine felt good as it slid down my legs.

GIA

I could hardly breathe. Chance was being led into the courtroom by two sheriffs. I was full of so much anxiety that I could have fainted right then and there. His attorneys had talked to me as we waited for his trial to start. They were confident. But I wasn't going to be convinced until Chance was coming home with me.

We hadn't talked since my last visit. I was still hurt. I couldn't even answer when he called me. I was still that mad. But I just had to be there for him. I didn't care if he was too stubborn to accept that I loved him enough to be there for him. If he didn't get it, he was going to learn that day. I wasn't going to miss his court date or any court date for that matter. I was going to be there for him until they didn't allow me through the doors.

Our eyes met as he walked towards the judge. I wanted to run towards him, kiss his face, and rip those chains from his hands and feet. He actually looked happy to see me. He actually smiled. I was happy that I could put a smile on his face. This situation was very gloomy and serious, but I still got cute for him when I got dressed that morning. I wanted to give him something to smile about.

He couldn't help looking back at me as the trial began.

"Your Honor, we'd like to submit a motion to dismiss all charges."

The state's attorney looked at Thomas like he was crazy.

Peter and Alex sat along each side of Chance at the table like his bodyguards.

"Based on what?!"

The judge lifted his hand to stop the state's attorney's outburst.

Thomas stood at the partition, confident and ready to plead Chance's case.

The judged asked, "Drop the charges based on what?"

Thomas answered the judge with a bunch of legal jargon that went straight over my head. In layman's terms, he'd explained to me that all of the evidence was circumstantial and that there was no concrete evidence to charge Chance with this crime.

"... Your Honor, even Simone Campbell, the other defendant in this case, denies Chance's involvement. She herself is free on bail. I ask that these charges be dropped against my client."

The judge looked at the state's attorney. "Have you discovered any other evidence in this case."

Regretfully, he responded, "No, Your Honor. But…"

"Then, upon the discovery of concrete evidence, you are free to re-charge the defendant. As of right now, the charges are dismissed."

I literally screamed with happiness. All of the sheriffs shot daggers at me to shut up. Chance looked back at me with the biggest grin on his face. My heart beat rapidly with joy.

I couldn't believe it!

Alex and Peter walked towards me as I stood to leave. When we met in the aisle, Peter threw his arms around me. Out of the corner of my eyes, I saw the sheriffs leading Chance towards the back.

"Where are they taking him?"

"He has to be processed. That will take about an hour," Alex told me as we left the courtroom.

"Then he can go home?"

"Yes, then he can go home," Alex answered with a smile.

I was so happy that tears fell from my eyes. I know that what Chance did was wrong. He took that girl's life, and he should pay for that. But at the time of her murder, he was so young, so lost, and so naive. He was just as much of a victim as Aeysha was. He lived every day punishing himself for that rash decision that he made. Ten or twenty years in jail wasn't going to help. His soul was in jail every day of his life anyway.

Peter put his arm around me as he led me towards the elevators.

"Thank you so much," I cried.

"It's not a problem, Gia. That's what you hired us for."

"We'll let Chance know that you will be outside waiting for him."

Even hearing those words sent excited chills down my spine.

I couldn't believe it. Chance didn't need to be locked up in a cell for the rest of his life to be sorry or rehabilitated. He lived every day, locked up in his guilt. He was sorry, and I knew that he would never harm another human being a day in his life. He deserved a second chance. And finally he was going to get that.

CHANCE

I couldn't believe it as I stepped outside of the County Building. I was wearing the Levis and white tee that I was arrested in. Unlike that day, my locs were fuzzy. I had mad new growth. I needed a fresh lining and shave bad as hell.

But I didn't give a fuck about any of that. No matter how rough I looked, I felt like a million bucks on the inside. It was almost three in the afternoon, so there was very little traffic going in and out of the building. I spotted Gia's white 300 sitting a few feet up the street with the hazards blinking.

Thomas was standing beside me. He'd stayed with me during processing to make sure that everything ran smoothly.

"Thanks," I told him as I shook his hand.

"It was our pleasure, Chance," he assured me.

However, he was hesitant. I knew that there was a lot he wanted to say. As my attorneys, they never asked me had I done it. They only asked me certain questions, because they said that they didn't want to commit perjury. But I knew what his look meant. The State could turn around and offer Simone the deal that they'd offered me. Knowing her, she would take it without thinking twice. And then I would be back in jail fighting for my life.

"I hope I never have to see you again," is what I told him.

He laughed, saying, "I hope so too."

He walked away, looking like Agent K from the Men in Black.

I wish he had one of those neutralizers to flash in my face to make me forget everything that happened in my past. As I walked towards Gia's 300, listening to the "Too Much" lyrics that spilled from her speakers, all I wanted to do was remember my future from that day forward. I was so sorry for killing Aeysha. I was so sorry for the pain that I saw Omari live with everyday. But I was dead too. My soul would never live freely because I would always remember that day that I killed her. I would live every day in pain because I punished myself every day. I lived in fear every day. I hadn't grown up in church, but I knew that God promised that I would reap what I sowed. I had sowed death. I lived everyday waiting to reap that.

♪ Don't think about it too much, too much, too much, too much
There's no need for us to rush it through
Don't think about it too much, too much, too much, too much
This is more than just a new lust for you ♪

Still, Drake's voice was like a breath of fresh air to me. I opened the door and the music hit me like the sweet breeze of freedom. Gia's face itself was like a breath of fresh air as she sat literally smiling like Chester Cheese as I climbed into the passenger side.

She squealed before wrapping her petite brown arms around me.

"Thank you, baby," was all that I could say.

She began to kiss me all over my face; my cheeks, my lips, my forehead, and, hell, even my eyes.

"What's all that?" I looked at Gia curiously after spotting a backseat full of luggage and bags.

"That's our stuff," she said nonchalantly. Then she smiled at me. "Where do you want to go?"

"Go?"

"We're out of here, baby. I have money saved up and a tank full of gas. Let's go and start over. Anywhere you want to go. If they want to charge you with anything, they'll have to come find you."

Just the thought of that made me relax in the seat even more. "Where are we going?"

"Where do you want to go?"

I sat back feeling the happiest I'd ever felt. The windows were down, so the warm air blew on my face. I couldn't believe how much I missed that simple feeling.

"Somewhere where it feels like this every day," I answered.

"California?"

"We can't drive to California. It will take us days and a ton of gas."

"Boy, I told you I got a pocket full of money!"

Just then, my heart felt like it had skipped a beat. I didn't realize how much I missed that wittiness and smile until that very moment. "Then let's go. California it is."

She smiled, and I caught her letting out a sigh of relief. She started the car and pulled off as I sat back, relaxed, and slid my hand onto her exposed thigh.

    I didn't grow up with a family that loved me. I didn't grow up being shown what love was. But I did know that sitting in that driver's seat was love in its purest form.

OMARI

I had been held up in Eboni's bedroom since the night before. For the life of me, I couldn't bring myself to get out of the bed. Eboni had been trying to feed me since I got there, but I didn't even have an appetite.

I couldn't wrap my head around all of this. I felt so bad for being so blind that I brought this crazy bitch into my life. I had been chasing Aeysha's murderer for a year, ready to kill him, when ultimately I was sleeping with the enemy and the person at fault was me.

I couldn't live life knowing that I had done this to my family. I didn't know how to live with this amount of guilt on my chest every day.

"Omari, you awake?"

Eboni's voice came over a round of light knocks on the door. I didn't say anything as I lay in the dark. I knew that it had to be the late afternoon. I was sure that the sun was still shining. But the shades were drawn.

Despite the darkness, I could see Jamari in her arms, along with someone coming in behind her. It was Capone, so I sat up.

He fussed at me as he flipped the lights on. "Man, I been calling you."

I squinted and groaned.

"Omari, get up. You gotta see this shit," Eboni told me. She put

Jamari in my arms. She had been doing that a lot since I got there- as if she was trying to show me what I had to live for. Capone had called her during the night to check on me and told her that he found me with a gun pointed to my head. She talked to me all night about what I had to live for, but I didn't talk back.

There were no chairs in her bedroom, so Capone sat on the bed next to me. "You good, bro?"

"I ... I don't..."

As I stumbled over my words, I noticed Eboni frantically fumbling with the remote.

Capone sternly put his arm around me. "Its all good, fam. We gon' get through this."

I looked at him like he had a third eye when he said "we".

He answered my curiosity. "Yea, nigga! *We!*"

When he laughed, I actually laughed too.

Then Capone told me, "And if you put yo' hands on me again, I'mma kill you myself." He was wearing a faint grin as he talked to me. He knew that I would never do it again.

I apologized, even though I knew that sorry wasn't enough. "I'm sorry about that, bro"

"It's good. You been goin' through a lot. You get a pass. *This time.*"

Having him by my side again actually relieved some of the pressure that I was feeling. My niggas was there with me, Jamari and Capone. They were my family. If my mother wasn't enough to live for, these two men were my reason to shake this shit off and continue to live. I had mouths to feed and people to take care of. I may have fucked up with one family, but I had a chance at another family to get it right. I just wished, with every fiber of my being, that I could have that second chance with Aeysha and Dahlia.

They say that everything happens for a reason. Maybe one day, I will know what that reason is. Until then, I would live everyday correcting my wrongs.

I could only pray that Aeysha was looking down on me, forgiving my stupidity but still proud for the man that I had become.

"Here it go! Here it go!"

I looked curiously at Eboni. She sat at the foot of the bed with her eyes glued to the television.

The television was on the channel nine news. Alicia Ramon was standing near what looked like a forest preserve.

She spoke unbelievably, as if what she was about to say had even shocked her. "We're coming to you live from the Calumet City Forest Preserve. Just a few hours ago, authorities were called to this location. A group of people celebrating a family reunion could hear the screams of a woman over the music that they were playing. They followed the screams inside the forest. Just a few feet into the forest, they made the gruesome discovery of a woman hanging from a tree by her wrists. Her body was on fire, the majority of her body completely engulfed in flames as she screamed for her life. Within seconds, the woman was dead. However, witnesses still attempted to put out the blaze as they called 9–1–1. Witnesses describe the scene as one from a horror movie, the smell of the burning flesh and the sounds of her gruesome screams as she burned alive, indescribable. An ID was located on the body. Though damaged by the fire, authorities were able to identify the victim as Simone Campbell."

The End...

Though this is the end of Simone, this is not the end of the Secrets of a Side Bitch series. Look out for new storylines and new characters in the near future! If you would like to get notifications of future releases sent straight to your phone, text the keyword "Jessica" to 25827.

Follow Jessica online:
Tweet Me: @authorjwatkins
Follow Me on Instagram: @authorjwatkins
Like My Fanpage:
www.facebook.com/authorjwatkins
Join the Jessica Watkins Fan Club:
www.facebook.com/groups/femistryfans

Made in the USA
Lexington, KY
02 September 2017